To

To all Best
wishes for a prosperous
future for you +
yours —

GASP!

Bruce A. Burton
+ family

GASP!

September Morning

A Sioux Detective Reunites Her Family In The Course Of Investigating A High-Tech Insurance Fraud.

Bruce A. Burton

Copyright © 1992, 2006 by Bruce A. Burton.

ISBN: Softcover   1-4257-0655-X

All rights reserved. No part of this book may be reproduced or transmitted in any form or by any means, electronic or mechanical, including photocopying, recording, or by any information storage and retrieval system, without permission in writing from the copyright owner.

This is a work of fiction. Names, characters, places and incidents either are the product of the author's imagination or are used fictitiously, and any resemblance to any actual persons, living or dead, events, or locales is entirely coincidental.

This book was printed in the United States of America.

To order additional copies of this book, contact:
Xlibris Corporation
1-888-795-4274
www.Xlibris.com
Orders@Xlibris.com
33057

For
Bruce and Hern

Ask, and it will be given you; seek, and you will find; knock, and it will be opened s to you. 8 For everyone who asks receives, and he who seeks finds, and to him who knocks it will be opened.
Mt. 7.7-8 (RSV)

The knocking continued. Kyle sat upright. He rolled off his cot, pulled on his jeans, wiped his eyes, raised the latch, and pulled the door open, and the cold air hit him in the face. A State Trooper stood in the dark, his cruiser rumbling behind him with its red light flashing over it like some space buggy.

"*Centradapoulis?*" the trooper asked, his face creased like a paper bag.

"Yes," Kyle answered, sudden heat spiking his spine because this same tall trooper, about sixty, his hair grey at the temples under his hat, once stopped him for speeding. The smell of the man's after-shave filling the doorway, Kyle squinted at his nametag in the faint light, then poked his head out the door past the dark uniform at his car reflecting the cruiser's red flashes.

"Your car?" The trooper pointed.

"Yes," Kyle answered, not knowing what the man could possibly want with his car.

"Expensive '69 Cobra—serial number?" the man continued, unmindful of the hour.

In the dark room behind him, the clock over Kyle's cot read 4:30AM. He pushed through the doorway and, the trooper following him down the short walk to the Cobra, he squeezed the door handle, pulled the door open, and reached inside the glove compartment for his registration. "Serial number."

"*Mrs. Chris Star* previous owner—" the trooper read under his flashlight from the Bill of Sale attached to the registration before folding it and handing it back to him. "Raise the lid, son."

Kyle felt as though he was being told to drop his pants, but he grabbed the lid, his grip, behind the air dam, reassuring him he owned the car. The chrome super-chargers and double manifolds on the 427 V 8 shimmered in the street lamp.

Passing his light over the engine, the trooper smiled faintly at the copper headers gleaming in the light. "This car has *a history,*" he mused suspiciously, "and, maybe, not the kind you're *banking on* when some high roller comes along—"

"*What?*" Kyle exclaimed incredulously, fear of losing his car twisting like a snake in his gut. "Those mugs aren't hiding anything."

The trooper snapped out a *Warrant and* handed it to Kyle.

A tow truck then rumbled up, backed up, and the Cobra's rear wheels rose indecently in the air. "If we don't find *anything*, you've got *nothing* to worry about," the trooper said, before ducking into his cruiser and shutting off the eggbeater. *"Stay cool, kid!"* The cruiser then went into reverse, and, its headlights disappearing down the road, Kyle stood there holding the ticket, feeling as empty as a sock. As he then watched *his car* also vanish down the road behind the tow truck, how he and Gail dreamed of their house at the lake last night hit him like a hammer blow—how happy she'd been, her eyes glistening at the lot they'd picked out overlooking the lake! Now *this collector's car, the sale* of the one thing that would make their dream come true, *was gone!*

Having lost all sense of time after the trooper seized his car, Kyle still hadn't called her at 10:30AM. He turned away from the Bronco and wiped the paint thinner off his hands with a rag. The September sun fell like neon on the garage apron. A red garbage truck roared past the body shop, smothering the street in black smoke.

What that trooper said about his car having a history nailed his shoes to the apron, and he was unable to move toward the phone. He hadn't said his car was stolen, but why had he asked to see the registration if he didn't suspect it? He'd sent Murph $5,500, all he could scrape together on his shop, to pay Mrs. Star, and Murph shipped the car by trailer truck out to him from San Diego. Had Mrs. Star, knowing how valuable the car was, *stolen* it and sold it *illegally* to him?

He was about to start for the phone when a black Cadillac drove up. He stood there for a moment, and then did a double take as a guy got out of the car, looked around the lot, and came toward him with a narrow expression in his black eyes. *"Don't see your car—"* the man, about fifty-five, puffed heavily, his leather shoes squeaking on the apron.

Caught between surprise and a gut dislike for the man, Kyle wordlessly shifted his weight from one foot to the other.

The man brushed his jaw with his thumb and looked out again at the nearly empty lot. He wore a rock-like diamond on his middle finger and a contemptuous expression, like a Halloween mask, on his face. "I said, *I don't see your car,*" he repeated.

"So?" Kyle answered shortly—

"*It's at the station—*" the man went on, flicking his gold bracelet.

"So?"

"You bought it from *the widow* of the guy who worked *for me* in San Diego."

"So?"

"Not curious about how he died?"

"Why?" Kyle answered.

"I'd like to buy the car." The man's soft leather shoes squashed on the apron as he stepped closer. "I'll give you *$20,000* for it." He took several bills from his wallet and gestured with the money at an old Dodge pickup in the lot, the shop's peeling paint, and its cracked cement floor. "You *need* the dough."

Kyle shook his head, knowing the car's value. The guy had something else in mind. He wanted no part of him. "It's not for sale," he said, turning away.

With large, sausage-like fingers, the man peeled another bill off his roll. His long greasy hair curved to a neat DA behind his ears. "Make it *$30,000.*"

Kyle faced the man, his throat hardening like Bondo. "*$30,000.* will buy a Sunbeam Tiger. Try *$800,000.*"

His black eyes tightening, the man briefly weighed the offer, then, his eyes measuring the younger man, he slid the bills back into his wallet. "Too steep, kid, after what *you* paid for it—"

Kyle's blood pounded in his temples, "That's no business of *yours,*" he said offended by being called *"kid."*

Unmoving, his eyes like steel, the man drew in his breath menacingly. "Oh? Well, I'll make it *my business.* Take it west, put money into it. Sell it easy. Divide the profits."

"I can sell it at auction," Kyle answered.

The man stepped closer to him, his breath on Kyle's cheek. He had thin lips and fang-like, yellow teeth. "Look, all you've got is a *broken down* shop, and a car worth a *little* dough, *if handled right.* Any other guy would jump at this."

"Let him jump."

The man took him by the arm. "You're not *hearing* me. Guys like you are suckers."

Kyle pulled away. *"Get out."*

"Mess with the *Altar Boy,* and you'll snap like *a twig,* kid." The man drew back, turned on his heel and walked back to the Cadillac. As he opened the door, he turned with a heavy voice—"*That car's my business. You people* don't own cars like that. *And stay away from her!*" He then got into the Cadillac, slammed the door with a hollow thud, and, spun out of the lot sending stones against the side of the shop.

Kyle leaned against the shop wall, boiling with anger. The man smelled like rancid garbage. He dirtied everything he touched. How could he have thought he would leave him alone? It might have been the car he was after, but he knew better now. His hands shook as he dialed *her* number. No answer, he hung up the phone.

"Got any bottles?"

Kyle spun around. A man in his late forties with grey-streaked hair, wearing a pullover and jeans, stood behind him, holding a tattered duffel bag. "John—" He swept half-a-dozen cans into the man's bag.

"Who tore out of here?" John asked.

"Drago."

John's eyes narrowed. "I saw your car at the police station—"

"Drago knew whom I bought it from," Kyle informed him.

"Can't hang on to *things,*" John said of the car with a shrug.

"I'm buying a house!" It took his every nickel to buy the car; he feared the poverty, which killed his mother. Without the car, he was in financial quicksand.

"*Quoyeh!*" John's lean figure tilted toward the ground, his eyes reflecting past realities.

"He told me to stay away from her!" he exclaimed.

John's eyes lit up. "What'd he say?"

"Said he'd bust me, if I didn't sell him the car. I told him, *no.* He said, '*stay away from her.*'"

"Sounds bad. I owned a red car like that—"

Drago said the previous owner died. And the color? A lot of Cobras were red. And how could John have owned it, if Murph bought if from Mrs. Star?

"If you had a Gremlin, no big loss," John laughed, deflecting his association with the car, adding, however, unable to detach himself from it, "but, as you say, you wouldn't have any prospects either, would you?"

"I bought it from Mrs. Star—"

"She must have gotten it after me. Don't mess with him."

"What do you know about him?"

"Slipped heroine into my car. Broke-up my marriage. I *did time.*" He had a far away look, loving the memory of his wife, as though he saw her image on the cement floor at his feet. "Her hair flowed like grass in the wind."

"Here—" Kyle fumbled with the pot on the table and splashed coffee into a cup, caught by this man's connection to the car. "When did you work for him?"

John took the cup. "Twenty-some years ago. I was about your age. He planted heroine in my car, the police impounded it, and someone, don't know who, got it at a police auction."

"Did Mrs. Star's husband work for him?" Two people had worked for Drago.

"Looks like it."

"Is it the same car?" Kyle asked in disbelief.

"You bought it out west—" John said.

"Yes."

"San Diego?"

"Yes."

"I lost my car there—"

Kyle scratched his head. "What happened to your wife?"

"Don't know—"

"He told me to stay away from his daughter," he repeated.

"He wanted my wife, too, I guess."

"Didn't you see her?"

"Her trail was cold when I got out, and she didn't return to her people—" he revealed painfully, not having spoken of it in years. "I thought she loved me," he added sadly, "but does it matter? He'll take you either way."

"Hell!" Kyle shouted angrily at the bizarre coincidence.

John walked toward the street. When he reached the sidewalk, a guy ran into him and knocked him to the pavement. Not stopping, the guy ran across the lot toward the shop.

"You don't want to sell your car, you little bastard?" He threw Kyle against the shop wall.

Kyle pressed against the wall and tried to stand. He half-fell when his arm gave way. He looked up at the guy's square jaw, pig-like nose, and shock of snow-white hair with a black streak running through it to his forehead like a skunk. He reached for a crowbar, but the man tore it from him and flung it out into the lot.

"You don't want to sell!" the guy repeated, his nostrils like red slashes in the side of an orange crate. Tires squashed the gravel. He stepped back to look.

Kyle leaned against the wall, his throat like sandpaper, black spots behind his eyes. He struggled for breath. *"Kyle!"* he heard, as he fought for consciousness with Gail by his side. "Whose your friend, Kyle?" She asked, sliding a 38 from her shoulder bag.

The snow-white head swiveled like a backhoe toward the gun. "Put that pea-shooter away, honey."

John stole up behind the man. Hs knife flashed in the sunlight. The man clutched his side and looked at the blood on his hand. "You touch that kid again and you're sausage—" John said.

"You *breeds* haven't seen the last of me," the brute growled, retreating.

Kyle's arm was heavy as stone as he felt Gail against him. He mumbled groggily. "Call the police, John . . ."

John slipped the knife under his pullover as the guy disappeared down the street. "He's gone."

"He hurt you, Kyle!" Gail exclaimed, her fingers on his arm. She had white teeth and full lips. She wore blue shorts and a blue ribbon in her blonde hair. "Your arm's broken. You've got to go to the hospital, Kyle."

His left arm hung limp. He winced under her touch. John gestured toward the car. "Let's get your arm looked at, *nephew*."

Gail's convertible swam in his vision. "Get rid of that car, Gail!" he blurted out.

Her eyes flashed. "It's mine," she said from some deep anguish.

"Let's get to the hospital before your arm falls off, Kyle," John insisted.

Gail held out her keys, her face flushed. "Take them, Kyle, and we'll be done with him." She picked a sheet rock knife up off the floor and slid it across her fingers. "I'll kill him," she whispered, as blood steamed from her hand.

"What are you doing?" He pulled a clean rag from his pocket and closed it over her fingers.

"He can't do this to us." Her voice came from a distance; tears of hatred welled in her eyes.

John pushed him to the convertible. "Get in, *nephew.*"

On their way to the hospital, her head lay against his neck, and he felt her soft thigh against his leg. The blood from her fingers seeped through the rag and stained her shorts; he pressed the clothe on her hand. She didn't move. His arm felt like it would fall off.

At the hospital emergency entrance, the smell of antiseptic threatened to knock him out. He sucked in the air as a nurse appeared and vanished with Gail behind a door. He half-stumbled after them. The nurse met him at the door; her starched blouse brushed against him.

"You can't come in," she said.

"She's my fiancé," he protested, seeing the doctor measuring a needle, and Gail standing against the gurney like a statue in a wax museum.

The nurse began to push him out the door. "He'll suture her up."

He pulled off his shirt. "My arm—" A point of bone stuck through the skin above his elbow.

"Oh—" the nurse said, exchanging glances with the doctor before leaving the room.

He reached for Gail. What hold did Drago have on her? If they'd grown up together, he might have known. He watched the sutures close the cuts across her fingers.

"Your arm, Kyle," she said softly, as though awakening from sleep.

The doctor turned to him. "Lie here." He lay on the gurney under a light. He felt the needle from the I.V. bottle in his arm.

"He broke your arm, Kyle, and you said nothing." She slid her hand into his.

The doctors noticed a wine-colored, moon-shaped mark on his shoulder as he lay on the table. "That's a rather prominent birthmark, son."

"My mother said I'd always be *recognizable*," Kyle laughed wryly

"And *our* children will be *our* honeymoon," Gail whispered in his ear, seeming to come right now.

He gazed at her, thinking her cutting herself was not like her, but an overcast moment. She was a flower again in the sunlight after a sudden rain.

The anesthesiologist stood over him. "Ok, son, tend to business, count— *one, two, three, four, five—*"

"He's ready for surgery," he heard, before losing consciousness.

He awoke in a hospital bed with John by his side. He spoke matter of factly, his eyes deep. "That creep *bumped* you, Kyle."

He looked for Gail in the room. "Where is she?"

John shook his head. "You awake? You've been mumbling."

The afternoon sun through the window cast an orange glow on the cast on his arm. He could feel where his arm had been broken. "Where is she?" he repeated.

"With *him*—"

The air went out of his lungs. *"Him?"*

"He took her from the parking lot—"

Kyle tried to reach across the bed. "Give me the phone."

"She's not there."

He slumped against the pillow. What happened? Why had he taken her? Why had she gone? "Did she resist?"

"Couldn't tell."

"Did she see you?"

"Think so."

John left the side of the bed and sat in the corner with a drum in his lap. His drumming floated hypnotically in the room. Kyle closed his eyes as John's drumming began to wander through him, soothing him and making right somehow the tremors about Gail not being there which shook him.

"Her trail is gone, washed away like after a rain," John intoned above the beat of the drum, as though he had foreseen everything; as though such shocks were natural, and one had to bend with them like willows in the wind or sand giving way under running water.

He remembered she said at Big Sur, the surf pounding and the fog rolling in, *'I'll tell you someday, Kyle. Be quiet now, knowing we love each other.'* Why hadn't she called to John? She'd cut her fingers, said she'd kill him. What had she meant at Big Sur about telling him someday? As he remembered what she said, he realized it had stuck with him over the last year. She had touched his black hair. *'You came from Athens long ago—'* What was she saying? What dark pool had that yellow butterfly hovered over? What wind troubled the dark waters of her spirit? His mind burned white with trying to remember some detail for the answer to what she had been referring to when she said she *'would tell him someday.'* How different from the certainty of their hours spent at the lake last night. He slipped back into them, into the quiet darkness filled with the scent of the hemlocks and the promise of a home together.

Flowing with the rhythm of the drum, he also recalled she loved to paint. Her paintings expressed their future, she said. She'd paint Paradise Bay from the hill where they planned their house. Her sense of the beautiful took form and texture on canvas. Her painting vented what troubled her, expressed something that had happened to her.

He started with a jerk, barely hearing the drum, but still responding to it, as if he was with Gail, feeling the pressure of her lips on his, her scent blending with the cedars against the sky behind them, the lake glowing in the sunset and the crickets trilling:

He lay on his side next to her, his weight mostly on the ground beside her. Her skin was slightly cool on the surface, but hot underneath. He pulled her close, hot and soft in his arms, her curves arching against him. She was round and yielding, full in his arms, and her scent so intoxicating he began to pass out, as if swimming through liquid gold, incubating, not hearing but hearing, the springs of life coiling and surging outward. And the darkness came with the dizziness, ascending, moaning inwardly, drawn into her, and coming together above that shiny yellow inland sea.

'*Say it,*" she said.

'*I love you*—' whispering. '*Even with your lips closed you talk. Everything about you speaks to me. See how you draw my strength out in a spawning way over these hills?*' Her hair was light and wet on his shoulder after their swim.

'*You body man*—' she said.

He dreamed: *The golden envelope, the seizure, and the water's edge, the twig beneath, its bark wavering ever so slightly, the warm sun, the grass so long and full under us, the cosmos filled with you, your bathing suit beside me close—your weight in climbing on, the unfinned mermaid wearing necklaces of pearls, vanishing by the millions over your breasts, the heave, the slow motion underwater thrust, spumes of bubbles sliding off in volume, disappearing into the watery body of the lake, the motion of my legs slowly straightening, breaking surface with groin lift as you're balanced on pushing vector, the slow-motion launch, that lift of ecstasy—*

He woke up. He didn't try to lift his arm. The drum held it down.

Why couldn't he discover her? His thoughts rolled against each other like leaves in the air, leaving him with the rustlings of small conclusions:

He could think of one thing and ask about several, used to be able to hold things in his mind without confusion. He had done that on the farm. He'd think about a problem while working, listen to the radio, and solve some problem. Not a great problem, but some problem. *The mind could solve anything,* he always thought.

He opened his eyes and looked out the window. The sun was down. "What makes you different from me?" he asked John, feeling angry, needing some wisdom, and wishing to hear his answer while he drummed. He thought of John's wife. "You never returned to your people, either. But, you're not swimming against the current." What wisdom prepared him for these shocks?

John stopped drumming. "I'm not alone as long as I have the *drum,* which keeps me in touch. If I didn't have it, I would be alone, alone and angry," he answered.

Kyle watched the declining light. Did John have faith in some goodness that kept him whole? What was he in touch with, the motion of things? How did he keep his balance? He closed his eyes, the drumming in his ears, blunting the narrow questions of her disappearance, blunting the pain of that reality; and he fell asleep to dream again:

Faintness, the wobble of the laggard's roll after exercise, somewhere in the middle ear we are connected with the earth, we are in tune, and we can roll anytime into sleep, dreams, into the drift of being, and then sleep when the ear turns our being to soil—oh, love's vertigo! All I need is love! Wonders profound, so powerful to lay between, the soles of your feet have little wrinkles, and your skin is the color of the sky—he saw the rippling lake and the trees towering in the moonlight over the roof of their dream house. He came to the surface like a swimmer, nearly unable to leave that gentle swirl in the depths of her private sea—

He left the hospital the next morning. He was at his shop making phone calls, trying to find out where Gail was, the assurances of the drum, before sleep yesterday, washed out by the bright September sun. Having no luck on the phone, he hung it up. He looked out the window, and the tow truck came in with his car hanging off the back of it.

"*The car!*" he said, turning to John with hollow excitement because he hadn't reached Gail.

"Maybe you keep it."

He had been trying to be cool, deliberate, in his attempts to find her, but panic rippled just beneath his skin. What good was the car without her? All he could see was her sitting there on the passenger's side. The car didn't make the ground firmer under him, though it was there. His eyes went over it. What was different about it? What had they done to it? The Cobra's side exhaust pipes gleamed in the September morning. It was rugged and spunky.

A man in a suit, John's age, got out of the truck, stepping lightly on the gravel.

Kyle met him at the apron, trying to keep the panic out of his voice to keep the car from disappearing again. "Everything okay?" Hope and fear struggled in his eyes.

"Kyle," the man handed him the keys, "my name's Wallace. I have a few questions."

Kyle's stomach tightened.

"You bought this number from a widow in San Diego, right?"

"Lieutenant Mitchell saw the Bill of Sale when he took it yesterday morning," he answered.

"Yes, it's in the car," the detective said, thumbing his belt. "Expensive car—"

"She didn't want it—" he quickly pointed out.

"You know her husband?" the man returned.

"No."

"His death was suspicious."

"Oh?"

"Hit and run."

"I didn't know—A Navy buddy bought the car, I guess from his widow. I didn't see anything wrong."

"Why didn't you drive it out yourself?"

"Not that distance. Besides, I was already here."

"You served on an Aegis missile cruiser. San Diego. Four years a target technician, right?" the detective asked, not accepting or rejecting his explanation as to why he didn't drive the car out. "I guess you're about twenty-eight years old."

"Yes, that's right—but did *eight* years in the Navy, not four."

"You knew then that Chris Star owned the car?" he repeated.

"No."

"That he was a *hit and run,* or Navy?"

"Navy? No, Murph bought the car for me. I didn't know either of them."

"Never saw him on your ship?"

"No," he answered again.

"How many on your Aegis?"

"Hundreds."

"You didn't know him?" The detective rubbed his neck, his eyes like an eagle's.

"No." Kyle turned to John, looking uneasy with the detective's trying to link him to Star.

"What do you want? He told you, he knows nothing," John said.

The detective returned to Kyle. "Sure."

John continued. "Why is Kyle's *Navy* important?"

"Star worked for Drago." The detective looked from John to Kyle.

"What's that got to do with me?" Kyle asked, feeling an invisible net tightening around him.

"Star was a naval engineer. He was on the same ship as you; owned the same car; worked for Drago. That's a string of coincidences." An expression of guilt by association crossed the detective's face.

"So, why did you take the car?" Kyle asked the detective.

"Drago filed an insurance claim. The insurance company called us. They traced the car out here on the claim. We found out the car was registered to Star."

"I don't get it."

"You're engaged to his daughter, aren't you?"

"Yes," Kyle answered, as if bitten by a live wire.

"How long?"

"Six months," he answered, expecting another shock.

"Where'd you meet her?"

"A bar—look, what have I done wrong?" he asked, filled with fear and dread, not knowing how she might be linked to this. Why she hadn't resisted when Drago took her from the parking lot. His arm felt like lead.

"Don't know if you're an accomplice or an innocent bystander." The detective smiled unevenly. "Maybe, you don't know anything. On the other hand—" he paused.

Kyle shrank back. Should he tell him Drago tried to buy the car? That someone attacked him yesterday? That Gail was missing? He felt like a hooked fish. "Are you going to charge me for something?" He couldn't understand the connection between Drago's claim and his car. "Does Drago claim the car is his?"

"No, and I'm not going to charge you with anything—" the detective repeated, leaving the door open to the possibility. "How'd you break your arm?"

"Shop accident." His skin darkened with the lie. He pointed at the Bronco behind him. "It slipped off the jack."

The detective glanced at the Ford, his face not revealing whether he thought that the answer was a lie. "This your business?"

"Yes," he answered, on solid ground with the truth.

"How long?"

"Since spring—"

"Mortgaged?"

"Yes."

"You're going to be married?" the detective probed unexpectedly.

"In a couple of weeks. I'm buying land," Kyle reasoned with him, wanting him to know that he worked hard and had done nothing illegal.

"That takes money—" the detective nodded, not waiting for a yes or no, but dropping the line in front of him. "Does she work for her father?" he asked.

"No—" Kyle answered, wanting to, but unable, to avoid the baited question. "She hates business—"

"Someone put something in the car," the detective revealed.

"The insurance people tell you that?" Kyle half-challenged, suddenly annoyed with his angling.

"Yes," the detective said.

"So, it's not the car, but something in it, and you found nothing?"

"They persuaded us to give it back," was all he said of the claim and the car.

"It's my car," he said.

"For the moment." The detective turned to John. "You did time for heroine possession. Found it in a car like this one. Star bought your car at a police auction after you were busted—It's the same red car, according to the San Diego police."

John's face tightened—"So what?"

"How long you know him?" the detective gestured to Kyle.

"Since summer."

"Heroine in your car got you into trouble. You were a mechanic in Quebec?"

"So?"

The detective looked at Kyle. "I could tear the car down to the rims," he threatened. "Turn that $1,000,000 car into scrap."

"But, the insurance company told you to give it back!" he protested.

"Maybe you aren't involved," the detective backed off, "despite the coincidences, and the fact that what the car is concealing is worth more than the car. You'll either do a stretch in the pen, like John here, or you have a clean $1,000,000. You're *Indian,* too, aren't you?"

"No," he answered, fielding the question.

"You two related?"

The detective's question rubbed his nerves raw. "No."

"You never used that heroine money, Eagle—" the detective continued, turning back to John.

John looked away, not hearing the man.

"I've told you everything," Kyle said desperately, burning to find Gail.

"I can wait." The detective turned on his heel. He stopped with his hand on the tow truck door handle and faced around. "Eagle knows what it's like on the inside," he said, gaining the seat and shutting the door.

The truck shifted gears out of the lot.

Kyle glanced at John, then threw himself behind the wheel of the Cobra, and snapped the keys hard. He shoved it into gear just as John came over the door and onto the seat beside him. He left black smoke in the air when his tires hit the street.

He ran up the stairs to Gail's suite at the Sagamore Hotel. Fumbling at the lock, he opened the door to an empty room. He went to the phone and called the desk: *No, the clerk hadn't seen her leave. No calls for Gail Drago all day.* He turned to John who stood silently, mentally searching the room. "She didn't come back last night," Kyle said.

"She never came back," John agreed.

Kyle went to the window overlooking the lake. A sloping lawn and islands of shrubbery stopped short of a line of trees and a boathouse on the water. "You said you thought the car was yours." He was unable to avoid recalling it now.

"Star got to it before Drago did, apparently, given Drago put me away. Surprised he wasn't there when they auctioned it off—"

Kyle took a deep breath. "Why'd he frame you?"

"I knew about his drug deals."

"He thought you were going to the police?"

"He got to them first."

"How'd you get messed up with him?"

"I met him in Canada. He offered me a job when he brought in a car to fix. Said he could use me out west. But, he was a crook."

"You run drugs for him?"

"He wanted me to."

"You think drugs are in the car?"

"No. He never got his hands on the car after I was busted."

"The detective said something's in it—"

"Something," John paused, and scratched his head, "maybe linked to the guy who worked for him—"

"Star?"

"Yeh."

"You never knew him?"

"No."

"So, we have the car—" It led through Star to him. It was a freak coincidence. He had the car, but not Gail. He stood there controlling his breathing. His eyes found the opposite shore across the lake. How often had he gazed at the lights twinkling in the darkness over there? How often had he followed the eastern mountains, curving against the sky, so unlike the raw mountains in the west? The weather had ripened them, rounded and matured them, and made poems of them. The cool lake lapped against them. They drenched the air with hemlock, pine, and ash. But, it was not as black as ink out there now with Gail's presence filling the room behind him like a few nights ago, but the stark midday reality of her disappearance, which blanched the window. That line of mountains, ending in the distance, now seemed to reveal her shape, and he longed for her. *"Where is she, John?"*

"You're following the points, *nephew,*" John said of his gazing, as he stood behind him. "Perhaps her trail is not so cold."

"We'll find her, won't we?" he asked for his help, unable avoiding thinking of John's failure to find his own wife.

"No, not like my wife—" John read his thoughts, his voice less gloomy than when he spoke of his wife at the shop.

His eyes picked up the mountains again. They loomed over both sides of Lake George for nearly all its thirty miles. Halfway up on the western shore, as he now recalled the scene, the Tongue Mountains reflected right up to the eastern bank; and the mountains north from Huletts Landing cast a ten mile reflection on the water. He and Gail had often gone there. She needed to paint that peaceful scene. The numerous fir, juniper, and pine-studded islands with low clouds, mist, and quiet water evoked Hokkaido, Japan. And, Putnam Pond in Chilson and many other Adirondack lakes had that same dreamy quality. He thought of her *'woodland pagoda'*; and her saying they would have one. Drago wouldn't have taken her to any of those places. No *Wasicun, Eater of the Fat,* as John called him, felt for the land and the joy it gave. Why didn't Drago want Gail to marry him? Why did he kidnap her? Why did the goon rough him up? It must have been for the claim, and not because he was a sucker.

He turned from the window and surveyed the room. He could hardly comprehend his situation. On the verge of his marriage, he stood in an empty room with a broken arm, wondering where she was, with the police breathing down his neck. No, she hadn't come back, as John said, for her boxes were stacked by the door like they were a couple of days ago. Braque's *Musical Instruments* was on the far wall, and an unpacked statue was on the table near the sofa.

He picked the statue, a replica of the *Phoenician Youth of Motya,* up off the table. She had said it looked like him. A minute ticked away. What she said of it was all he had of himself in her room. It was the only evidence that they had plans together, that they even knew each other. One minute she was here, the next, she was gone.

"He looks Native, *nephew,*" John said of the statue, "if it had hair like yours, it'd look *Native.*"

"That detective thought we were related," he replied, caught by the oddness of John's observation. "Doesn't that strike you as odd, since I never saw you before this summer?"

John shrugged. *"You look Native."*

He held up the naked statue. It was lean, tough and manly young—he himself looked younger, even acted younger than he actually was; yet, that detective had guessed his age right: twenty-eight. But, after the last day he felt like eighty-two. "Why do I look *Native?*" he asked, aware more than ever of the mystery of his past.

"Long face, long hair. You're supple as a wishbone. You were adopted. They brought you from out west to that farm above the lake, *nephew.*" John reminded him.

"Yeh," he said, remembering having mentioned it. He laughed at the absurdity of it.

"Think of the drum."

"Trying to make me think like you do?" The drum soothed him though. "The drum talks to everybody."

"No."

He tried not to be annoyed; he was trying to find Gail, his own past, now of no importance to him. "Let's not guess about me."

He walked into her bedroom. Sheets and blankets were folded on her bed. Lilac perfume permeated the room. He looked out the window into the parking lot behind the hotel where she parked her convertible. "Drago drove off in her convertible, didn't he?" He figured John saw the car.

"Yes," John answered through the door.

He disliked that convertible, and hadn't been sure until now why, or, why he so strongly disliked Drago. He wasn't going to deny anything now that he might have avoided before. He hated Drago because he owned a computer company, talked hard, was unclean, and bullied people, like he bullied him about the car. John told him he was a drug dealer, and the idea of Drago and computers was like stirring snake oil into a punch bowl. His claim, whatever it was, had to be dirty, too. But, he couldn't get the car. He took his own daughter. Drove off in the convertible. It was like he was taking back what he thought was his. What he tried to do, and what he did, was foul. "I should have told that detective about him."

"He'd have suspected you all the more. He half-does already."

"You know Star, who owned the car?"

"I told you I didn't."

"What's in the car? Why suspect me?"

"He's not leaving anything out."

"It's fucking crazy. Sick and crazy. I wish you'd told me about him."

"None of my business."

"We're both in it!" He felt sick to his stomach. How could she have a father like that? Would it have made a difference, if he had known? No. He still would have fallen in love with her.

As he stood there, a grey Acura with California plates followed a cab to the curb below the window. A woman with red hair, wearing jeans and a sweater, and a man in jeans and a tweed jacket, got out of the cab and disappeared under the window into the building.

"Gail's college roommate's here for our wedding." How could he face her?

"*Kyle!*" Candy exclaimed at the door in what seemed like only seconds.

He reacted awkwardly, embarrassed at her finding him here like this, and stepped wordlessly back.

"*What happened to you?*" she asked.

He lifted the cast self-consciously. "An accident," he said, "this is John Eagle, Candy."

Candy nodded to John. She had a pleasant oval face—

"I see Gail's moving. Where are you going to live?" her husband said of the boxes near the door.

Candy walked to the window, half-listening for his answer. "*What a view!*" She turned and looked around the room. "*Where is she!*"

"Gone." He didn't drop his eyes.

"*What?*"

"Missing." He choked on the word.

"*What!*" Candy came toward him. "*What are you talking about?*"

"*Her father abducted her!*" he blurted out, unable to hide it.

"Drago, her stepfather?"

"*Stepfather?*" He felt like she touched him with a cattle prod.

"He's not her father." Candy looked surprised he didn't know. She averted her eyes.

"What're you saying?" he asked, not understanding.

"He's *not* her father, Kyle." Candy spoke firmly.

"I didn't know—" Had Gail tried to tell him that at Big Sur? "Who is her father?" He felt his way among the thorns like a blind person.

Candy stood by the table with a pained expression on her face. "He died when she was little after Viet Nam. Drago married his widow. I thought you knew."

He stared at her, a sickness growing in him

"She didn't tell you?" Her eyes told him she was feeling for the harder places in him.

"Her mother died—" Drago, her stepfather? Jesus! The blood drained from his face. He almost knew what was coming.

"Kyle, you look pale."

Monstrous, half-formed shapes Gail herself recently suggested on a drive into the mountains loomed before him. They'd parked in a picnic area and viewed the birches where she liked to listen to music. He'd pushed in *Swan Lake*, and the brooding music flowed out of the car. Her eyes brimmed with tears, and she touched his arm. *'He's capable of anything!'* Her *stepfather,* not her father! At Big Sur, she said she'd *'tell him someday.' 'I never want to tell you, Kyle.'* He'd cradled her head in his arms because she was in pain. *'He can't do any more to mother, Kyle.'* He looked at Candy. Her eyes revealed what he suspected. "Tell me," he said evenly, his voice sounding dreadful to him, standing to receive the blow.

"Call the police!" she said instead.

"Say it," he mumbled, asking her for what he didn't want to hear.

She came close to him. "He told you to stay away from her—"

His eyes told her to tell him.

She stood poised like a diver on the board with a reluctant expression in her eyes.

"Say it," he choked, not thinking of murder, but something as bad.

"She prayed you wouldn't know." Candy finished, not saying exactly what it was.

"Her mother knew—" He stood on the edge of the unspeakable, realizing something her mother couldn't face made her kill herself.

"Yes."

"Say it—"

Candy's face revealed anguish and pity. She remained silent.

He sat down. "When did you find out?" he managed to ask, nearly without breath, suffocating, his lungs frozen in his chest, his throat in a vice.

"That night you met in the bar. It happened again."

He slumped back onto the sofa. She picked a flower. His throat closed. He looked vacantly around the suite Drago paid for. Now the convertible, the car that keep her quiet, blanketed the secret, made sense, *'take it and we'll be done with him.'* He gathered his strength and stood up. He seized on the California car following the cab. "Who followed you here? They with you?"

"Who?"

"That Acura behind you—"

"No, we're alone—"

"I have something to do—" He could barely lift his injured arm when he reached for the doorknob.

He didn't hear John follow him out of the suite, but, in the parking lot behind the hotel, Candy and her husband looked down from Gail's bedroom window at them. What Drago was, was clear as piss. "She never told me. How can I not love her the more, John?" He wiped the hot tears from his eyes. The secret twisted through him like a corkscrew. *"Jesus,"* he gasped. He twisted the wooden wheel hard.

John touched his shoulder. *"Nephew'*, we'll find her. But, what's in the car is the branch pointing the way."

"Yes," he said hearing, but not hearing, *"the broken branch."* The shattering of innocence.

The auto-body shop with its two brown overhead doors sat at the back of the lot. The September sun drenched the maples hanging over the building. Fall was in the leaves; their yellowing was warm, gentle, and acid-like in the air.

Deep sadness engulfed him. He had met Gail in fall. She was his melancholy, his 'sickness,' his open sea, his peace and fulfillment. He longed to point the Cobra anywhere—as long as she was with him, and they could heal together—put the pedal to the floor and never look back. He didn't care about the shop he would leave behind. He was a sailor, a dune runner, facing the red ivy and yellow sumac dying against the gray shop wall, yearning for the open sea or the desert and to live in peace with her; if only he had her; if only he knew where she was—

The shop was closed and silent. Like an old acquaintance, it smelled of premature age; but it was his shop, his business, and his future until now. It made buying land, a log house for her, only her, until now, possible. Thunderheads of doubt and uncertainty towered over his future.

He sat behind the wheel, the Cobra's oval-grill breathing close to the gravel, waiting for John to open the overhead. When it opened, he snapped the car into gear and drove into the shop. Inside, the car took up little floor space, but it was big with a problem, a secret attached to death, a secret affecting his love. He got out of the car, not knowing where to look or what to look for; but he had to remind himself, not to let his sick anger smoother him. He had to be cool.

He leaned against the bench. "Where do we start?" he asked, trying to muster the strength, wanting and needing to see *the branch* clearly, now that he knew the worst that had happened, not allowing himself to think what was happening to her now.

John shook his head. "I don't know, *nephew*. It's not like engine work. Tell me what to do. But, remember, don't let love or hunger blind you. It's the only way to see."

"It was *your* car—" He wanted to cry like a child struck by the sad irony John wasn't even able to find his own wife.

John spoke firmly without possession, his voice hopeful. "It's your car now, *nephew*."

He tried to think as a whole person to measure himself against the task. He tightened his gut and counted his strengths: his mechanical ability, being able to drive anything on wheels, being good at math and cross-word puzzles, able to work computers, and his gift of solving problems by insight. His flair was in his brain and his fingers like Theseus, not in his brawn, arms or legs, like Heracles who slew three-headed dogs, though the man he faced was worse than a three-headed dog. "I have heroes," he said, feeling ludicrously weak.

John smiled to relieve his young friend's pain. "*Quoyeh!* Sitting Bull, Crazy Horse! Anything to help find what you're looking for!"

He needed John's strength.

"Learn from them!"

If he gave of himself like Theseus or Pericles, Sitting Bull or Crazy Horse, he could possibly do what was required. He positioned himself before the car, knowing he needed patience, the gift that allowed him to figure out how to rig a car clutch, or make a new hand-tool on his lathe, or rewire a defunct tape deck. He was not after a great triumph over the world, only a victory of mind over Golub Drago, who stunk of Croesus's wealth and the foulness of Diomedes' flesh eating mares: a *Wasicun, Eater of the Fat,* like John said, who plundered, killed, and raped.

He pushed the pain aside and gazed at the AC Cobra Ford. The police had found nothing. What were they looking for? He had to be logical, systematic. There were mathematical regularities in life; certain things were predictable. Science and technology allowed weather forecasting. You could track a target based on electronics and calculus.

What was different about the car? He was conscious of John's eyes upon him as he moved from the bench and began inspecting its tail, bumper, and lights. He surveyed the body from the side, lingered over the paint, the polishing. He knew every inch of the car. How often had he gone over the rounded body after each coat of paint, or wiped the protruding chrome headlights, or windexed the small arched windshield? And that air-scoop on the lid feed a points and condenser supercharged V-8 with eight open headers.

This was not an electronic fuel-injected engine—just a black, barrel-shaped engine set in the chest of a beetle-sized, fire-blowing two-seater, squatting on chromium mag-wheels. The car was tough. Two men owned it before him, John and Star, the dead man. It had been to the Threatening Hill. It would take him to that Hill where you *'hit the wall,'* where you either prevailed or were defeated. The car held a secret, and it would have to give it up; but he would ask it as a friend. He didn't want to have to tear the car down, regardless of what it was worth. The car was not his enemy; it only contained the secret to Gail's freedom.

Think logically and instinctively like an engineer, like Star who planted some secret in the car, he reminded himself. The man had sat in the same seat and worked the same gears. He pictured a bald engineer, a good mind behind the wheel. He didn't know why or what he had planted in the car, or what his connection was with it. Only knew he worked for Drago. Yet, he would have felt the solid pull of the engine through the gears. Where, if he wanted to hide something in the car, would such a man hide it? In front of him, where he could see it? Under his seat? Behind him? Jesus, who knew?

He looked through the inside of the car. He felt under the seats; let his fingers glide over the curves and creases where leather met steel. He contoured the dials and the dash with his fingertips, snapped the switches, and checked the heater. He wanted the car to feel the awe in his fingers, so it would *'speak'* to him. He resisted feeling powerless, resisted hating the unknown forces, which tore at him. The car had to tell him what he wanted to know—

What more did he know of Star? What had he left out? The cruiser, naval engineer. If on the Aegis that meant missile systems. He worked for Drago in San Diego. Drago owned a computer business after John knew him. If the car concealed a chip, no matter how small, he had to find it. But, chips were smaller than a fingernail! And how did he know it was a chip? Maybe it was a process; maybe it was something to do with math.

"What have I fixed, and what needs fixing in the car?" he asked himself aloud, taking a different tack, his voice echoing in the shop. Only the odometer needs fixing, he silently realized; it had never moved since he owned the car. It always read the same numbers, *'69696.9'*. He would never forget those numbers. For some strange reason they were burned into his brain.

He rolled the creeper under the Cobra; thought of Drago made him sweat, and fear and anger began to marble his purpose. Sweat ran into his eyes.

Why had Drago allowed the car to go east? Why wait these weeks before trying to get it from him now? Apparently, he didn't know whom Mrs. Star sold it to, until Murph shipped it out here. He also missed the police auction when Star bought it. Or, she may have told him weeks later; or, not at all, and he saw it for the first time here in Lake George. Either way, Drago was certain it was the same car because of how he questioned him, his saying an employee had a car like this one. Yes, he knew it was Star's car. And Drago knew Star put something in it because Drago filed a claim, and even the police searched the car. But why did Star do this, if he worked for Drago? He had no answers.

The cast on his arm was awkward under the car, but he disconnected the speedometer cable and pulled it from the transmission. John stood next to him as he inspected it under his bench light. "It looks all right."

John looked at it. "Yeh."

He studied the cable more closely. "So, why is the dial frozen?" he asked. "Did the odometer work when you had it?"

"Yes," John answered, "maybe the needle's stuck. Maybe it's stuck in the transmission, rusted or something."

He tapped the dial—the speedometer worked. He knew that already. Only the odometer was frozen. '69696.9'. But, that never bothered him, the odometer reading on the Bill of Sale was the same as when Star owned the car; but, it was ridiculously high mileage, or was it? Why hadn't he ever gotten around to fixing it? He didn't know—just natural inertia, he guessed. You never did get to all the things you thought you should get to. Even so, he couldn't see why the odometer didn't work, if the cable was okay. He went back to the bench and leaned against it.

"Must be rusted—" John repeated. "Road salt."

His eyes traced the random cracks in the cement shop floor near his feet. Did these cracks hold some clue? No, frost made these cracks in the floor. He couldn't get to the problem through indirection. He was at a loss.

He began to wander more deeply into the problem, and found himself in a thicket of speculation. Scientists thought a Chaos Paradigm of seemingly random events governed the workings of the universe; they called it natural law, which they thought they could discover with super computers; the law that they thought might even govern the workings of the Stock Market. He read about that theory, and he wondered about it—

"If scientists found the law of Chaos, they would know the mind of the Creator, and I would be able to find what is in this car," he said aloud, John still there with him. "Do you have the notion of Chaos, do you have the notion of 'accident'?"

"*Accident* is part of the natural way of the Creator and the Earth-Mother—" John said.

He groped like a blind man down a corridor. He would welcome the Creator or the Earth Mother guiding his fingers to the doorways and windows. Something told him he should know what was in the car, what connected him with Star, a guided missile engineer, for there had to be knowledge and thought in what he did. He tried to think in straight lines, but only drew disconnected curves. Thought of Gail threatened to overwhelm him. "I need a clue."

"Look to the Earth Mother given his offense, *nephew,*" John observed of his look. "Give yourself to the problem. You are the offspring of the Creator and the Earth Mother. They are both in you."

The Earth Mother. The Creator. *The Chaos Paradigm.* The female substance of the universe; the androgynous design. Drago offended nature; offended what conceived life itself; offended its purpose. He had to be guided by the female principle. John and instinct told him, he should approach the problem with joy, not anger, to receive the solution. He had to 'marry' the problem; let it absorb him. But, he didn't know what he looked for. He stood in darkness. He had no context. If he looked for numbers, they would have no context; numbers without a context wore the face of Infinity. The cracks in the floor, like cobwebs of dust, had no pattern. They were not like spider webs with designs and centers.

Did the problem have a solution? What if he couldn't find what he was looking for? He began to doubt himself. *No, I won't do that,* he thought, starting to panic as the sun sank behind the trees across the street, sending slanting rays through the shop, illuminating the red Cobra in a blaze of light. The wooden wheel drew his hands. The leather seats invited him to sit down; so, he sat in the car and gripped the oak wheel, feeling the pressure for action mount in his body, imagining the cold air rushing through the cockpit. "I need to drive it," he said, looking up to find that John had left.

He heard the rumble of an engine outside the shop and got out of the car, his train of thought broken. He opened the door on a tan Mustang parked in the lot and a woman stepping out of it as though out of a dream. Her jeans hugged her thighs like *Saran Wrap.* In her forties, she had long black hair and chocolate-colored eyes.

Kyle rubbed his eyes. He reacted as though he might have been standing on the deck of his cruiser and been knocked off balance by a sudden wave. A woman with a *'67 Mustang?* Yes, the cars were scare.

The woman moved fast. One moment she was stepping out of the car, and, the next, was talking to him.

"I'm closed," he said, though drawn to the car.

"Your door is open," the woman observed of the overhead, her eyes sharp, not bothered by getting '*no*' for an answer.

The Mustang vibrated in its own engine heat. It wasn't faded. It didn't need a paint job. He wanted to get back to his own car. "Can't do it," he said firmly.

The strange woman reached into her leather shoulder bag. "How much do you want?" she asked, undeterred by his refusal.

"$5.00," he answered to get rid of her, since she insisted.

"You're working on that *Cobra.*"

"I don't have time for yours."

She smiled oddly, enigmatically, and handed him a $1,000 bill. She wore a turquoise bracelet and rings. "I'll come back for the car tomorrow," she said, her business done.

"Park it." He wouldn't argue about the job. He'd call a cab to get rid of her. But, she stood there looking at the Cobra, as though she had seen the car before. She was here for some other reason than a paint job. He hesitated, about to ask her what she really wanted, but decided against it. He walked into his office, dialed the phone, spoke, and hung up. The woman looked out onto the street as though expecting someone. In a few minutes, the cab arrived, pulling up in the glory of its yellow rust. She seemed to undulate in the fall sunset, like a poltergeist above the Mojave dunes, when she walked away from him toward the cab. He thought better about taking her money. He followed her and handed the bill back to her through the cab window. "You'd better keep this 'til the job is done." He tried to find some point of connection in her black eyes.

"Honest," she only said, stuffing the money like a piece of *Kleenex* into her bag. She spoke to the cabbie and the cab drove off.

He pulled down the overhead. He picked up the speedometer cable again; then got on the creeper and rolled under the car for another look. He had a fishy feeling about the transmission. He didn't know why. But, the frozen odometer and the cable sparked something in him. His injured arm felt like a stick of wood and began to ache as he lay there on the creeper, looking up under the car.

Following intuition, he traced the rough surface of the transmission housing with his fingers, as if the car was flesh and bone, not steel and bolts. He closed his eyes against the falling dirt as he cleaned the housing with a wire brush. He held a mirror up to it. He couldn't see the surface in the mirror, given the narrow angle between the housing and the body of the car, so he got a pencil and paper from his office and made a rubbing of the grooves.

At the bench, he studied the rubbing. The numbers did not identify a *Ford Motor Company* part. His eyes rested on the Mustang and the possibility it had similar markings.

He went out to the car to bring it into the shop. The keys hung from the ignition, but his fingers froze on the door handle. Instead of getting into the car, he popped the lid. The engine held eight carburetors and two rows of four bronze tumblers, like the Cobra. What did she want with a souped-up car? Was it wired? Something told him to stay out of it. Something told him the car was booby-trapped. Ice creep through his veins.

He got a coil of wire from his shop and connected the wire to the ignition and unwound the coil back to the shop and closed the overhead. He looked at the car through the overhead window, reluctant at the last moment to touch the wires—

The explosion knocked him to the floor. Black smoke and the smell of burning rubber engulfed the shop. He lay on his back amidst the shattered glass and scraps of metal, feeling like he was floating through space and eternity. The clock in his mind stopped as he blindly, slowly wiped the dirt from his face, his hands covered with blood.

Then he was dimly aware of sirens tearing at the air and of a trooper's red eggbeater slicing through the smoke above him and fire engines pulling up to the burning Mustang. He rose on his elbow. He couldn't see the street through the smoke of the burning car. A man ran toward him, his knees going up and down as though riding a bicycle. That same detective who questioned him earlier stood over him.

"I'm all right—" he mumbled, not knowing how badly hurt he really was. What could he tell this detective? That a woman he didn't know tried to blow him *to the other side?*

The detective picked up the wires leading from the smoldering car. "First your arm and now this. Bad luck follows you. Shit! *Why* did you wire the car?"

"A feeling," Kyle answered, dusk filling his eyes as the firemen jitterbugged around an opaque fire that consumed what was left of the car.

"Whose car is it?" the detective bore down on him.

"A woman's," he answered, beginning to cough with the shock of the explosion.

"You're in somebody's way, Centradapoulis." The detective looked back into the shop. "Where's Eagle? Was he here when this happened?"

"No." Kyle wiped his eyes. The overhead doors and his plate glass office window were blown in, but the Cobra, parked close to the bench, was undamaged.

He lay there on the verge of passing out with the detective's voice sounding like it came from a hollow log.

"Star worked for Drago. He was killed in San Diego," the detective stated. "Didn't I tell you that?"

"What are you talking about?" he asked numbly, not understanding what the detective meant.

"The insurance company tells us Star left a note. You have his car. It's a rolling coffin. Can't you put 2 + 2 together?"

"No—" He began to see the fire fighters, not dancing now, having shut out the smoke from the car.

"Are you all right? You sound groggy, got an ugly cut on your head."

"I'm alright." He tried to make sense of what the man was saying. What did he mean, *a note?* Blood tricked down his nose. He wiped it across his cheek. His mind clicked back to Murph, and to how he himself got the car by accident. "A Navy buddy shipped the car out to me," he repeated. "I don't know anything about a note," he said, trying sit up straight.

The detective grasped his uninjured arm. "You knew all along there was some property in the car, didn't you?"

"No." He slumped back against the wall, his chest tightening.

"You served on the same cruiser with Star."

"I never met the man—" he protested. "I told you that."

"Who wants to *knock you off?*"

Shock gave way to anger. He stood up unsteadily. "Look, there's nothing in Star and me on that cruiser," he coughed. *"I never knew the man!* He was about to spill about Drago, but remembered John said that the detective would suspect him the more. *"Believe me, Wallace!"*

The police radio crackled in the detective's cruiser, and he walked to it through the smoke. The traffic began to move on the street as cars passed like metal turtles beyond the burned out car. The detective had a hard look in his eyes when he returned. "The *CBI* in San Diego says your buddy's been murdered. Did he know computers in the Navy, too?"

Kyle's insides churned. He'd done his stint in the Navy with Murph. Nights together in Subic Bay in smoky bars, having a few drinks were like last night. He and Murph were *brothers* when neither of them had a brother.

"I'm a bystander." The smell of burning rubber and exhaust blended with the smell of spent leaves. He felt sick.

"Star hid something," he heard the detective say. "That insurance guy show up?"

"No—"

"You didn't know the woman who owned this Mustang?"

"No—"

"What she look like?"

He only remembered her turquoise bracelet and rings. "I don't know—" Her image flashed before him—"She had long black hair."

The detective paused. "Never saw her before?"

"No."

The detective turned away. "I'll put out an APB on her. What else about her?"

"Nothing." He wiped his face and closed his eyes.

Not getting any more out of him, the detective left.

The shop fell silent. Kyle gazed at the wheels that were all that was left of the blown out Mustang. He stood up unsteadily in the last rays of light with a wrenching in his gut. Would she come back and finish him off? His knees shook and he could barely stand up. He yearned for the woods or some back road where he could hide.

He got into his car and stiffly twisted the key. As he backed out, the glass and metal on the floor from the explosion crunched under his tires. A last ray of light in the mirror revealed a long gash across his forehead—

He pulled the Cobra into his driveway after midnight, the rain bouncing like pebbles off the windshield. He didn't bother to cover his car, but left it open to the rain and, the strength back in his legs, ran through the puddles to his house. He stopped short when he noticed lights on inside. He craned his neck at the window to see who might be in there, and, through the wet glass, saw a *minisuper* on the table by his cot. *'Who would have brought that?'* he wondered, as he twisted the doorknob.

As he jumped just inside the door Gail's CD player clicked on filling the room with flute music. The melancholy sound held him like John's solitary drumming in the hospital room, draining the tension, and fatigue through his feet, and filling him with visions of the western desert with dunes and cactus and a fiery sun. His steps creaked across the floor toward the kitchen where he paused on the threshold seeing the woman who had brought him the car. She stood at the stove with her long black hair falling over a red sweater to her waist. Her back was to him. She spoke without turning around. "Thought you'd be hungry."

The smell of sizzling burgers hung in the low room as the rain beat off the roof. He was hungry, but it was not a gut hunger, but some spirit hunger the flute awakened in him. If he had to die now in his own kitchen, he would welcome it. She half-turned as thunder echoed over the lake.

"What are you waiting for?"

He stood near her at the stove, looking at her Asian eyes and a face that might have been carved from walnut. Cypriote women had long lashes and fixed brown eyes like hers; he'd also seen such eyes in the west. "You're native—" he said to her.

"*Sioux*. Are you Sioux?" She looked him straight in the face.

"No," he answered.

"Who's your friend?" she asked.

"What friend?"

"The one who thinks you're Native?"

"How do you know that?"

"You're honest, the kind of man who makes friends. A friend would say it." She noted the cut on his forehead. The strangeness of his finding her here dissipated. "Well, who is he?" she asked again, her tone softening.

"A guy from up north," he only said.

"If you're not a Native, what are you?" she asked evenly again, showing no further interest in John, only focusing on him.

"My parents name was Centradapoulis." He tried to keep himself from being lost in the unexpected turn of her questions.

"Sounds Greek. You were adopted?"

"Yes, it's Greek. What does it matter?" After meeting Gail, following his parents' deaths, he gave up trying to find out about himself. Her bringing it up now annoyed him. Yet, here he was talking to her about it.

"You don't look Greek." She smiled faintly.

"I'm not a Sioux, if that's what you mean. Did you try to kill me today? Did you wire that car?"

She dabbed cold water on the cut on his face. "No."

He felt like a leaf eddying in the circle of her surprising concern. She was like an old friend; yet, he had never seen her before today. "Someone wired the ignition," he revealed, feeling he could trust her.

She motioned him to a stool by the counter. "Sit down." The thunder over the lake and the flute music imbued her with a special quality. She held his gaze. Her breathing tightened slightly, and she closed her fist on the counter. "When I shut off the car it armed the bomb. I should have known. It's not the first time someone's tried to kill me. I didn't realize the danger, not thinking they could find me so quickly, which is why I always carry this—" She opened a leather bag by her stool and laid a semi-automatic P-85 Ruger on the counter.

She spoke like a pleasant dream beyond memory. He looked at the pistol, struck by the incongruity of her manner and her lethal caution. He struggled with the possibilities of Drago's trail of bodies. What could he do? He had to trust this woman. Perhaps, neither Drago nor the white-haired guy had murdered Murph, given the timing, but either of them could have killed Star. Either of them could have tried to kill her. Instinct assured him she was not involved with Drago. If she was telling the truth and had to carry a gun, then he could trust her.

Lightening flickered in the back yard through the window above the sink. The lilac bushes rolled in the wind. He thought of Murph and his taking care to ship a valuable car out here to him. He flopped like a flounder on the sand. "Who are you?" he asked.

"I'm with the insurance company. Didn't Wallace tell you I was coming?"

"He mentioned something about a *'guy'*."

"The person who tried to kill me today—and almost killed you—" she went on, "is likely the same person who killed Star and your friend Murphy." She spoke slowly, so as not to be misunderstood, so that he knew she knew what was going on, and that she didn't suspect him in the fraud. "Star developed an equation for the fracture strength of the silicon for a micro machine a fraction the width of a human hair. Such machines will clean out cholesterol, scour tubing, and destroy cancer cells some day. This device, when developed, will be worth $billions. Star hid the equation from Drago, and took money from European interests, without being able to deliver the equation to them. *The clue to his equation is in your car.* Drago filed a claim on it. That's why I'm here."

"How do you know this?" He wanted to confirm what the detective told him about the insurance company getting a note from Star.

"Star's widow sent us a note from her husband."

"Why would he keep the equation from Drago?"

"Drago leveraged Star's computer company with drug money. It was Star's way to get even. He wasn't about to hand Drago an invention he'd worked on for years."

"A white-haired guy tried to muscle the car from me yesterday."

She fell silent. She slid her hand down the butt of the Ruger and looked into his eyes. "That white-haired guy plays for keeps. You were lucky to get away with only a broken arm."

"*Drago took Gail yesterday afternoon while I was in the hospital!*" he exclaimed banging his cast on the counter, unable to keep the anguish out of his voice.

"Oh?"

"Yeh! And that detective links me with Star on that cruiser. But, I never knew him!"

"Relax, I know about your Navy. I brought a minisuper," she said, seemingly passing over Gail's abduction.

"Our being in the Navy's only coincidence," he kept on with her since that was what she was here for—

"Things happen that way."

"Chaos," he then agreed, suddenly realizing he shouldn't struggle with this woman.

She knew enough about him to bring that computer he saw on the table by his cot, didn't she? If what she said about Star's letter was true, the numbers meant something, but what? "Look," he said, pulling the paper with the transmission numbers from his pocket. "I found these on the Cobra." He never heard of micro machines. He didn't know about such chemistry, physics, or engineering. He wasn't a biotech engineer, just a sailor with a blank past who punched numbers onto a screen.

She held the paper with the numbers. "There's a computer connection with your target work."

"You know a lot about me."

"There's much I don't know."

"What do you mean?"

"I know little more than what you know," she said, alluding to his adoptive past. If she knew anything else about him, she wasn't saying, rather kept focusing on his connection with Star and the Navy. "You know how to operate a system."

"Star's missile system?"

"Yes," she said, leaving the kitchen for the living room.

"You have some skill, some knowledge," she repeated next to him at the mini super. "This machine will plot a trajectory. That must be the connection because Star designed the system you operated on the *Aegis*. Forget the fact it's a coincidence, unless—" she paused, as if suddenly realizing something, "Star knew you and wanted you to have the car."

"How could that be?"

"He had to have known Drago's daughter. Knew she was seeing you before he was killed."

A light glowed in his mind. The car was not advertised. His widow did contact Murphy. Star must have known he and Murph were friends. Murphy said she wanted to give it to him, *'Look, she's a widow, so give her $5,500 for it.'* So, that's what he'd done. He didn't reveal to the agent that he now thought the car *was* intended for him. He went on to the problem of it, his mind buzzing like a fly against a light bulb. "What do missile trajectories have to do with molecular space? Micro machines are molecular, if they can clean out cholesterol!" He was suddenly eager to punch the numbers into the machine, though the machine differed from the computers he had operated.

"Don't think about cholesterol, this is math and machinery, not biology. There is logic, and Star put the clue to a machine in a machine; and now you know it, too." She took as certain Star intended the car for him, her face expressing satisfaction.

"What kind of a machine is this? I've never used one like it." A processing board of green lights lit up on the side.

"A vector machine that'll do gigaflops," she said.

"Groups of numbers—"

"Billions in a second—"

"A *number cruncher*—"

"But, not big enough for your genome," she said wryly.

He gazed at the machine worth three times his car.

"Wake it up."

He sat at the keyboard and punched in the numbers. The monitor flashed up cubes and circles on the screen. They interlocked, rolled, and dissolved—then new circles and cubes came up, only to roll and dissolve across the screen again. The unconverted numbers were oddly familiar, but, like someone's name on the tip of his tongue, or someone's signature he should recognize, he couldn't grasp what they meant. "They're not crunching."

She studied the paper. "These numbers are incomplete."

"They're not part numbers."

"No, they're not."

"Why, if this technology is so valuable, would Drago kill the engineer who invented it?"

"He found out Star cut a deal with the Europeans, as I told you, and that the numbers were in the car. Figured he could get them out himself. But, he was wrong. Star's widow gave us his note and contacted your friend. Drago is a coyote."

A plot had formed around him like the shell around a chick, and he had been as oblivious to it as a chick. He tried to think. There had to be other numbers in the car. But, where? He folded the paper into his pocket. "What did his note say?"

"He didn't tell us where the numbers were, if that's what you mean."

"Just that they were in the car?" His mind began to turn—the dial on the dash glowed in his mind.

"Only that, so Drago couldn't find them."

"But, he wanted the equation deciphered." He thought of the frozen odometer. *'69696.9'.*

"Without Drago doing it."

"He thought Drago would find out?"

"Yes."

"So, he wrote you that the numbers were there, and didn't say where. He thought I could do this?" He was flabbergasted. But, now he was sure he had the clue. *"Wait!"*

"What is it?"

"Without the other numbers, the computer is useless, right?"

"Yes."

"The odometer's frozen."

"Punch in the numbers then," she said.

The keyboard clicked as he punched in *'69696.9'*. Nothing happened. The screen keep rolling and dissolving like before.

"Good try—" she said, barely masking her disappointment. "Thought you might have had something there."

He flipped the switch on the mini super, and the monitor went black, leaving a pale light from the window on the table where dim dawn crept into the room.

"We have a long day ahead. We need food and sleep." She walked back into the kitchen characteristically undeterred.

He didn't move from his chair. He felt stupid for jumping at the odometer like that and coming up empty-handed. What was he going to do now? The situation threatened to overwhelm him. But, he had to still act, he couldn't just sit there in dumb amazement either at his own stupidity or at what she revealed. He drummed his fingers on the table. He did have part of the key in the numbers he'd already found. He was certain of that. Those numbers off the transmission meant *something* to the computer—but still, they were, as she said, incomplete.

So, where were the others, if they were not on the odometer as he had so quickly thought? He mentally began to search the car again, his eyes drifting to the window where dawn grew after the rain; but, the window was empty, and his mind began to go blank with lack of sleep. As his eyes closed, a tap on the glass jerked him awake and John came in the door, his long hair wet with his being out all night.

"I saw that Mustang."

"Someone tried to kill an insurance investigator. She's in the kitchen. Where'd you go anyway?" he asked wearily.

"To talk to Wallace," John answered.

"And?"

"It was my car alright. Whose the agent?" His eyes fastened on the ajar kitchen door.

"Forgot to ask. She brought this." He gestured at the mini super.

"What is it?"

"A vector machine. A *number cruncher*," he answered almost indifferently.

"Oh."

"But, I found—" he began with renewed excitement—

"What?"

"Numbers on the transmission—"

John scratched his head. "No phone call from her?"

"No—" he then answered miserably.

"*Wasicun,*" John said between his teeth at Kyle's drawn appearance. "I smell food, let's get some."

They went into the kitchen and when the woman saw John she dropped the plate she was holding on the floor.

"*Shirin!*" John exclaimed, suddenly clasping her to him.

The couple wordlessly held each other in the middle of the kitchen while, dumbfounded, Kyle picked up the hamburgers.

"*You're not dead, John Eagle!*" she whispered against his neck, trembling in his arms.

John looked at her. "I looked *everywhere* for you—"

"He tried to kill me after your arrest. But, I kept him from getting the car!" she explained her hiding and why he couldn't find her.

"Kyle, this is my wife!"

"What, John!"

John didn't bother explaining more to him, only spoke to his wife. "Kyle's red car is our old car, Shirin! The one Drago planted the heroine in!"

"*Quoyeh!*" She looked at Kyle.

"You didn't know?"

"No, only that the police had it when I drew Drago off the auction. I never knew who bought it."

"Well, Kyle got it from a widow after Drago leveraged—"

"Her husband's company—" she finished for him.

He looked deeply into her eyes.

She put her fingers on his lips to silence him. "I am still looking," she said quietly. "After your arrest, he chased me. I left him with a woman. But, when I came back for him, he was gone." Tears welled in her eyes. "I tried to find her."

"And?" he asked.

"*I never found her.*"

"What was her name?"

"She was white and childless, is all I know." She searched his eyes for his understanding.

"No one knew her?"

"No one."

"But, *you're* safe!"

"*We must find him!*" she said almost desperately. "*I cannot forgive myself—*"

"But—"

Tears choked her. "*You think it wasn't my fault?*"

"It's all right," he said, comforting her, holding her. "Kyle follows the broken branch for *his* woman!"

"I know," Shirin wiped her cheeks, "we'll find her, too, my husband."

"*Ah!*" Kyle exclaimed, not knowing what they were talking about, but feeling he was standing on the edge of a cliff where Drago was concerned. "*Is there no one he hasn't touched?*"

The next morning, Kyle bolted upright from his cot and sprang to the door: the Cobra, wet with the top open, was still in the driveway. *How thoughtless in not covering the car!* he faulted himself, thankful it hadn't been taken while he slept. He then realized the house was cold; he smelled bacon cooking and coffee brewing from the kitchen.

He went down to the kitchen and found the back door open, and orange September, bearing the smell of last night's rain, blazing through it. It would be hot. He longed for Gail, her scent, and her soft breath against his chest. He washed his face at the sink and rubbed his eyes dry with a towel, the fall morning filling him with such yearning for her, death would have been welcome with her in his arms. He walked by the stove and the swimming bacon, feeling tired, his nerves ragged.

Shirin and John were outside on the back patio. Shirin sat in an aluminum lawn chair, looking at a map. Kyle went over to them.

Shirin laid the map aside. "John thinks they're in Quebec."

"I first met *coyote* in Perce'," John informed him. "No one sniffed the car last night—" he added, no trace of tiredness in his face, wanting Kyle to know he had kept his eye on it.

"I shouldn't have left it in the rain like that. Why is he in Perce'?"

"He was running drugs up there when I met him. Didn't know it at the time," John answered.

"He wanted John to be his west coast link after the feds began shutting down Florida," Shirin said.

"So, you think he's gone back there—"

"If he's on a kidnapping rap, he's safer out of the country," Shirin continued.

"What do we do?"

"You've got the car," she said.

"He took her to get it!" he said hoarsely.

"He wants the equation, as I told you."

"Did you tell her the rest, John?" he asked with anguish of what Candy disclosed yesterday.

"Shirin, that *Wasicun*—" John began.

But, there was a knock on the door and he didn't hear what she said as he went through the kitchen into the living room. A *Federal Express* agent stood there with an envelope in his hands.

"Kyle Centradapoulis?" the agent asked, handing him a clipboard with a pen.

Kyle's signature jerked across the invoice, and the man handed him the envelope. He tore it open. He held her blue kerchief, smelling of lilacs, up to his nose, inhaling the scent he'd just been longing for.

Shirin came up behind him and took the envelope and read the address on it. "I guess he's up there," she said

Kyle thrust his hand into the empty envelope. "But, there's no letter, no note—*nothing!*"

She pointed out the address. "Look, *Gaspesie.*"

"Should we go up there now?" John asked.

"And have him bushwhack us on the road?" his wife asked. "No, not so fast, John—" But, she was obviously still trying to decide.

"Yeh, we'll be moving geese all the way," John agreed, "and, he tried to kill you once, Shirin."

"Twice," she corrected him. "But, that bomb, yesterday, was a mistake. Even the police had to trace the Mustang because the insurance company didn't tell them who was coming. The thug who beat you up checked it out and the police told him—I think he nailed the car just on the plates."

"You don't think Drago knows you're here then?" Kyle asked.

"He might know. Maybe he'll bargain, if he knows."

"But, he tried to kill you!" John exclaimed.

"But, he wants the equation now. So, if he knows I'm here, he knows I'm after it, too, and that maybe I'll get it. And he saw me drop the child. He had to have paid the woman. He'll trade information about him for my giving him the equation, if we find it."

"And if we don't find it?" John asked.

"Drago won't know that," she replied. "That equation, real or unreal, is our passport to Canada."

"He *paid* her?" John clasped her arm.

She nodded. "And he'll bargain for the claim, or what's in the car," she repeated. "It's our only hope."

"How does he know *anything's* in the car?"

"When he filed the claim, a guy in the office told him, since Star had worked for him. He didn't see anything wrong, telling him about the note."

"And Gail?" Kyle asked.

"To lever *you,*" she said. "You not only got the car, but he added 1+1 and came up with the Aegis system. Drago's not stupid, though I should rephrase that-he's *criminal cunning* like a fox trying to get into a hen house."

"And where is that white-haired thug?"

"Don't know—" she answered.

"You told me last night, you met him before, Shirin," John revealed.

"New York," she declared, eyes expressing pain.

"Did he kill my friend?" Kyle asked.

"No, not him, but some one working with him. But, that white-haired guy killed *Star* when he hid the numbers."

"So he works for Drago?" Of course, how else could Kyle explain the attack?

"He works for Drago," Shirin confirmed. She pressed her eyes closed with her palms as though resigned to the inevitability of meeting that guy again.

"When do we leave?" Kyle asked suddenly filled with impatience. However, his impatience was tempered by her posture. Was she really concerned about meeting that guy again, or was it something else? He didn't know what private hurt she was hiding, but he knew it was something great, something that had to do with Drago—with that child she spoke of to John, maybe—Perhaps, as a man, he might possibly never understand or know what she suffered. It was something in her past, something connected with her womanhood. She filled him with pity and a strange sorrow as he observed her sitting there with her palms over her eyes, as though she might be crying and not want anyone to see. But he could only stand there helplessly.

"*Now*, I guess. We leave now. There's nothing to fear from him if he thinks we have the formula," she said with resolution, her eyes incredibly sad.

"I'll gas the car," Kyle said barely able to continue beholding the awful suffering and power of this woman.

"Take your scatter gun," she advised him, drawing her breath deeply, not having missed his double barrel in the kitchen closet.

"We can't all go in my car," he pointed out.

She thought for a moment. "John'll take the mini then."

"Why John?" he asked, suddenly fearing being separated from it. "I can take it in the trunk."

"They'll be after the car—it'll be safer with John in your truck—we have no choice," she replied firmly. "If we lose the mini, we're sunk."

"You still think we'll find the numbers then?"

"Possibly."

"Okay, John takes the pickup."

Kyle dropped John at the shop. The Mustang was where Gail had parked her convertible two days before. He shrank from the memory of the blast while he dialed the junkyard to tow it away. He hung up the phone. John sat in the old Dodge ready to leave to pick up the mini. He turned the key.

"Just take it easy," he cautioned, "it runs all right, but it's old. It's full of gas."

John looked at the gauge. "Right." He looked at his friend. "Kyle, she found me."

"*It's a miracle.*"

"The mind of the Creator. The drum and the Earth Mother. The Circle must come right again."

"But, you gave up hope."

"She had enough for both of us," he smiled. "Remember the Creator is in us. Knowing that should keep us from being foolish. It kept the drum in my hands. Maybe, I really hadn't given up hope. Maybe, I knew in here," he touched his chest, "she'd come back."

"Does it direct you?"

"It *inheres* in us. It is what we are."

"You're a philosopher," he said, trying to understand.

"No, Shirin's husband, and a father."

The old truck coughed once, and he hit the accelerator.

John's renewal, his words, soaked up some of his desolation. And, Drago did make contact. He sent her kerchief. It brought horror, but hope, too. It was a scent, direction, something more than the undecipherable numbers in his pocket that he had yesterday.

As he got into his car, a tan *Jaguar* appeared across the street. He pumped the Cobra into the traffic. The Jaguar came into his rear view mirror. His hands sweated on the wheel and he wiped his palms. Up the street at a gas station, a Transvan, on the other side of the pumps, hid the Cobra from the street. He filled the tank.

The Jaguar held back in the traffic behind him. Would it tail him back to the house? He turned on Mohican for the mountain road above town. Halfway up, the Jag didn't reappear. If after he picked up Shirin and had to race the Jaguar, he felt confident he could outrun it.

The Jaguar reappeared. He downshifted and hit the accelerator. The Cobra jumped like a goat on the tarmac. He up shifted and sped along Mohican, leaving the Jaguar the empty road. He sped on for a mile, the lake, below the road, shimmering through the trees in the mid-morning sun.

The Jaguar didn't reappear in his mirror, so he turned right down the mountain back into town. He put the car through a couple of hard turns and neared his house. A *959 Turbo Porsche* was behind the trees in his driveway. He didn't see the Dodge. Alarmed, he drove into a neighbor's driveway bordering his back yard. He grabbed his shotgun and ran across the yard.

The kitchen was quiet, but water ran in the upstairs bathroom. He stopped to listen. Shots suddenly ripped out and the bitter smell of gunpowder blew through the house and stung his nose. There was fighting upstairs, and John came falling down the stairs. Kyle grabbed him by the arm.

"*He's back again!*" he exclaimed, jumping up.

The whole top floor seemed to be caving in—there were more shots and the wood splintered off the banister. The house was engulfed in grey-blue smoke and Kyle coughed.

"*Come on!*" John shouted taking three stairs in one jump.

Then someone ran down the hall to the right upper bedroom. A tongue of flame snapped against the bathroom door.

John was half way up the stairs when Shirin dodged ahead of him down the hall into the bedroom. The three of them stood in a cloud of acrid smoke. Kyle felt the house was about to burst into hellish sulfurous flame. He pressed his face against the cracked window glass. They watched the Turbo screech out of the driveway below the broken window. Exhaust from the car wafted up over the porch roof and through the window where they stood. Shirin had her Ruger up, and then lowered it. She held the smoking pistol at her side. "*He didn't hit you?*" she asked John.

John looked at the window casing, the glass, and at the blood on the sill. "No, but he left a piece of himself."

"He's carrying a *Glok*—It's him all right," she breathed heavily.

Kyle's fingers stuck to the stock of his shotgun as he walked back to the bathroom. Shots through the door had shattered the bathtub. His legs felt very light, as though they weren't carrying him.

"The coyote who broke your arm, *nephew,*" John said, standing next to him.

Shirin bumped his elbow. "A good thing you're taking the mini, if he tries for us on the road."

"Where *is* the jalopy?" Kyle asked.

"Next street."

"A Jaguar tailed me," Kyle said, nearly forgetting the car.

"Did you lose it?" Shirin asked.

"Yes."

"They'll be back—"

"Who?"

"Star's disappointed *Europeans* probably. He sold to them rather than have his equation fall into Drago's hands. Gave the money to his wife. But, he wasn't able to deliver. Some compensation for his company." Shirin went to the top of the stairs. The house was beginning to clear. "We can't sit here any longer."

They were half way down the stairs when the phone rang. Kyle listened to the voice, concentrating on the message while trying to determine if Drago spoke through a handkerchief. He couldn't tell. The receiver went dead. His heart pounded like a sledgehammer. *"Gaspésie! A gas station in Percé."* Kyle gasped. *"Those were the instructions."*

"It has a mini-mart," John said.

"Kyle and I'll take the mountain route and overnight at your camp in case we're set up," Shirin said to John.

He hesitated. "Why not let the police bag him for kidnapping?"

"He won't talk in jail. We want the boy."

"What boy?" Kyle asked.

"I'll tell you later," she answered.

"Can you find the place?" John asked, surprised for some reason Kyle didn't know.

"Yes."

"Let's go then!" Kyle said impatiently.

She grasped his arm. Her black hair lay heavily on her shoulders. "Don't be impatient, Kyle."

John took his elbow. "Be smart, *nephew.* Listen to her, *Quoyeh!"*

Shirin put the mini into two canvas-covered cardboard boxes. After John left with them, they crossed the back yard to the Cobra. He opened the trunk and she flung in her duffel bag. They then headed north from Lake Shore Drive onto Horican. Lake George fell away when they snaked up toward I—87, Exit 24. He went over the speed limit. The Dodge appeared ahead of them. John waved them by.

The Cobra ate up the empty road. Shirin turned her bracelet with its large turquoise stone, as big as an oval moon, on her wrist and spoke softly. "Slow down, Kyle."

He eased back on the pedal, relieved to be on the road, giving himself to the car's power and welcoming doing something. After the last thirty-six hours, he sniffed the air like a paroled prisoner.

Shirin slipped a tape into the deck. A haunting flute echoed her careful manner, as if telling them that, if you were caring and deliberate, it lessened the pain of your loss and gave hope it might come out all right. The music was delicate and involuted like Gail's paintings. As he sat behind the wheel feeling the Cobra's power, he understood, as much as a person seeing a mist lifting off the upper reaches of the lake might understand, what her paintings meant to her. They expressed the yearnings and the secrets of her womanhood, and, if he had been more alert to that, he might have understood that she had been hurt; or that what took *'life'* in her forms and colors were distilled wishes, dreams, and poetry, what was right, wholesome, lyrical, her only compensations for what had happened to her. She painted to tell him this, giving him something gauzy and almost Asian that thrilled the spirit, revealing the fertile, natural woman she was, those soft and yielding roses and flowers. *'I want our lives to be art, Kyle.'* And how, had he, as a man, been nearly oblivious to this? Maybe, John meant this by being of the Earth Mother. Gail was of the Earth Mother. He never thought of it that way before; but, what else could it be?

His hands tightened on the wheel, and the windshield blurred in front of him. He sucked in the air as it rushed over the top of the car, understanding now what she meant by wanting their lives to be art. She taught him and loved him, and he now only wanted to hold her and tell her he understood; that he wanted to know, as completely as he could, as a man, her hopes and desires, and her purpose as a woman. She was a universe and he needed her. They were mutually receptive; he knew her design.

"Gail tried to tell me—" he began, uncertain as to how to say it, thinking of the other as taking and hating.

"I know," she said, her eyes closed. "Women are rarely heard. Only other women hear what they say. But, it's a language all can understand."

"I want to learn."

"If you're true," she said.

"How?"

"You do for *all* like a warrior."

"I've been stupid."

"Unmindful of the important thing."

"Ah, yes, *things.*" He spoke ironically.

"*Wasicun things,* you mean."

"Yes, I jumped at this car."

"Mrs. Star didn't need the money. She just wanted to get rid of it. But, you thought you could cash out with a $1,000,000. car?"

"Yes."

"It runs—" She smiled. "John used to flatten it. It feels good to be back in it."

"Do you actually think you'll find this *boy* you're looking for?"

She pushed back against the seat, her expression revealing that she was feeling the flute and the car's power. *"E'yayo,* he's my sister's son!"

"You know how it's going to come out?"

"I do, and I don't," she replied enigmatically. "I've been looking for him for twenty years."

He didn't know what she meant, or why she was looking, or what happened to her sister that she felt she had to look for the boy. He wanted to ask, but just being with her buoyed him up and gave him hope, lifted his depression and impatience. He looked in the rear view. "Can I hit it?"

"Why not?" she answered. "The car's mated to the road. It has its own medicine."

He pushed his foot down. The needle popped up to 70. A red eggbeater then whipped from the bushes after them. He downshifted and went onto the I-87 ramp. The *Yield* sign flew past, and he hit the pedal again, and the sucking super-chargers blending with the flute, pulled him back against the seat and made the roadside pines and hemlocks whizz bye. "The police," he said, wanting to really push it, wanting to feel the car's power and go with the spinning universe, leaving the police in his wake.

She turned around. The cruiser came out on the Interstate behind them. An almost child-like smile flashed across her face. *"E'yayo!—"*

He took a long curve and sent the cruiser to a vanishing spot in his side view mirror. He didn't fear being stopped by the police. Nothing, short of a roadblock, could stop him. The car had the wings of an eagle.

Then, the tan Jaguar did a U-turn behind him on the other side of the Interstate. It slid out of sight behind the trees as they sped by. *"That Jaguar, this morning!"*

She turned around, the smile still on her face. The tan car reappeared. She opened her handbag and pulled out the Ruger, loaded it, and cocked the hammer. "Let them come on, Kyle, then give it the reins and leave the *Wasicuns* in your exhaust!" Her hair flowed over the back of the seat.

He lightened the pedal and the tan car grew closer. He had never felt such a surge, like the spirit of the west with a hundred Sioux war ponies pounding the asphalt ahead of him. "I can't blow a piston!" he cautioned, poised over the pedal, driving with his good hand, his foot eager and heavy to press.

"You won't." She watched the tan car come after them. "John would have blown it long ago, if this pony was going to break. *Okay!*" she shouted, as flame flashed from the Jaguar, and bullets ripped through the door near his elbow.

"Jesus!"

"Put his belly on the ground and let the coyotes howl—"

His foot pressed heavily on the pedal, and the supers sucked the warm September air, sending the red car up the Interstate. There was no limit to it's speed, no limit to the strength of the heart that beat in its chest—he then heard an odd sound coming from the front or the dash of the car like the whirr of crickets outside the sound of the engine—and then, like a sudden stillness, the odd sound and the excitement were gone when the coyotes flagged and disappeared after a few more miles down the road.

"Too many valves, John would say." She said of the Jaguar, looking back, a note of satisfaction in her voice. "How fast did we go?" she asked, referring to the Cobra.

"We must have topped 200. Look the needle's down to 160 now." The thrill of that burst of speed was still in his legs.

"Take 73 to Saranac Lake, Kyle." She flipped the tape over, her eyes thoughtful. "We'll get off at Pottersville."

The Cobra plunged off the Interstate at Exit 26, and Kyle pulled onto Route 9 and downshifted.

"Head for Olmstedville—"

"Who was that bastard at the house?" he asked, suddenly thinking of the guy who attacked her there.

"Didn't you know?"

"I only saw the Porsche."

She brushed her hair back, her turquoise rings picking up the light, and looked at the road, her lips firm. *"Stick,* the white-haired guy." She hardly paused with her directions as though he and the attack were not important now. "At Olmstedville the mountains are open in any direction."

He eased off the pedal. The V-8 hummed quietly. She was quiet; just turned her bracelet. He'd let her think about how she wanted to answer, her obviously knowing that he needed to know something of this guy. But, he grew calmer and concentrated on his driving.

He took the left to Olmstedville as the sun began to sink in the western sky. The coming night gave him solace because it would hide the car. They drove through Olmstedville and approached 28N where he pushed the Cobra on a stretch of empty road. The *Adirondacks* were like the backs of enormous bears, and he drove right up between their shoulders.

"Gas up at Winebrook Hills. After that, take any right turns for Lakes Harris or Rich."

She wasn't going to answer him now, he thought. "You know the way."

"I've been here—" she said simply, her teeth even and very white, her eyes clear, their dark expression open and clear.

At dusk they were on a winding dirt road strewn with stones. The dark sky outlined the trees. The road wound several miles into the forest, and, where it ended abruptly, they parked the car. Shirin picked out her duffel bag. "We'll walk the rest."

He followed her in the dark. She blended with the spruce and hemlock, moss, earth, and water of the woods. He tried to see in the dark when rocks caught his heels. Then the path rose abruptly; but they didn't pause, until, at the top of the path, they reached a cabin perched on a cliff overlooking the lake. Catlin stretched northwest in a quiet glow into the distance. Standing there, he re-experienced the isolation of his missile cruiser at sea, the lake recalling the greenish glow of his tracking screen. He felt the paper with the numbers in his pocket. How could he find the other numbers at night? He stood there for several minutes, waiting and thinking, as she went into the cabin. A dim light came through the window.

Inside, a field stone fireplace took up one log wall. Two chairs obliquely faced it. Paintings on the walls of clouds, animals, and people wearing feathers emerged from the dim light. One was a portrait of Shirin dressed in a red cloak, wearing two blue and white feathers in her hair. Another painting was of John and Shirin standing together under a blue and yellow sky in the glory of fall. John held a peace pipe and wore red leggings with a blue and white belt. Shirin, in headband and feather, wore a white dress patterned with pink and white flowers under a red cloak. They appeared to be in their twenties.

Shirin observed him studying the paintings in the dim shadows. "Our marriage—" she said.

" John was not homeless—" He realized how little he knew of the man, and how little effort it would have taken to find out about him.

"We are never homeless in our own country—His father was a fisherman. His mother taught the Micmac language. They hunted here in winter."

"Are his parents alive?"

Not answering, she collected some paper and wood, her movements deliberate, calm, assured. A fire sprang up the chimney.

"John disappears sometimes. Guess he comes up here—but, I thought you'd never been here before," he continued.

She laughed in a small way. "I came here once because he spoke of it, stayed as long as I could, but he never showed up until at your house. Things work that way—"

"You just missed each other—" he said, still trying to figure out the way things worked. For a moment, he was back in his shop looking at the cracks in the cement floor, thinking about the Chaos Paradigm. But, he was beginning to see it wasn't Chaos, but that something else that Gail expressed; what John spoke of.

"Yes, just missed him," she sighed, turning her back on the small kitchen.

"Why didn't you leave him a note?"

"For some coyote? It worked out better this way—"

"You've got Drago and your sister's boy in your sights."

"Yes," she said with deep eyes. "When did you meet your girl?" Strangely, the way she asked indicated she wanted some confirmation of what she knew.

"After a long stint at sea," he said simply, "in a San Diego bar. She wanted to leave California, and I had to sell my parents' farm."

"So, you came out here—"

That night in the bar with Gail reminded him of how frightened and tense, lonely and frightened and tense she was. "Yes, and Drago's a bastard."

"Before taking Star's company with drug money, he drove a garbage truck. A small time hood, he moved over to drugs. Wasn't long before he was in Canada developing a route."

"*Wasicun.*" He used John's word, unable to keep the bitterness out of his voice. She had studied Drago, knew about him for a long time apparently.

"Now it's a $1,000,000,000 fraud on a micro machine he doesn't own. Coyote's at the rabbit hole—" she said.

He thought of Gail's apartment. Thought of her being with Drago filled him with horror. Moonlight fell across the floor. "And Stick?" he asked, the pain in his upper arm reminding him of him, asking her again.

"He killed a woman in Brooklyn nine years ago," she then revealed.

"You've been in insurance that long?"

"Following Drago. Come on." She slipped a white feather into her hair and left the cabin.

He followed her out the door. They sat on the dark, quiet cliff overlooking the lake. As he gazed across the water, a loon called and a fish jumped, breaking the greenish-yellow glow over the water. Her profile was soft in the moonlight, her eyes deep, her head bowed toward the water with the eagle feather glowing against her hair, filling her with grace and power, knowing things about the earth without which nothing was created, nothing breathed, nothing came into this world—things he was only beginning to become aware of.

A large owl flew close; he felt its feathers and the power of its glide. How close had he actually come to entering the owl's world when younger in the woods, or, when, on that missile cruiser, he lost himself in the hypnotic churning Pacific that kept the ship afloat? How close before coming east and loosing innocence, loosing the ability to trust? How close might Gail have come to the same source, if, as a child, she could have kept her innocence? Thought of her threatened to crush him. They kept her pregnancy to themselves, taking joy from it, knowing only they knew, and, now, she was with the hood she hated more than any other person in the world. Would she use the gun? Would they ever sit on the edge of such a lake as this, witnessing such wonder together?

Shirin dropped the line and seemed to hold the moon in her hand. The loon called again across the water, and the night became as still as eternity with the moon suspended in it. "What are we going to do?" he asked, unable to keep the desperation out of his voice, looking at the woman looking at the water, moving slightly, and drawing up a wagging, silver-striped trout, as if by magic, laying the fish by her side, she and the fish seemingly inseparable from the night, the lake, the earth, the moon, her movements, shape, and smell, sound, and touch, making the earth and its creatures a thing of sisterhood.

She touched his arm. He felt a mother's energy through her fingers. "Power and money sickness possess him, and will close his circle, Kyle. But, you, no matter how hard it gets, always have a good thought, for that is the healing way." She searched his eyes, and, as she looked across the lake, the moonlight gave her skin a soft, yielding quality. "The way of the Earth Mother is a power greater than any Wasicun coyote's, who thinks he can put the moon in a jar or this lake in a dish—"

"Greed—" he said, repeating her. She spoke like his stepmother.

"*Graed*, sick hunger—" She stressed the word. "The cruel feudalism that knows no race, which cripples women."

"Mother Teresa said *'there are no great triumphs in life, only small acts of love,'*" he said, caught up in the night.

"Tell me of *your* mother." She looked deeply into his eyes.

"She grieved," he revealed.

"Oh?"

"But, she loved me—" His stepfather caused her grief. He'd treated her harshly; yet, she managed to teach him respect for women. That's what he felt for Gail. *Respect.*

" Your mother was a fine woman—"

"She said *'wealth was striving after wind'.*" She reasoned her despair, he realized, as he sat there. His stepfather turned violent not having money. So, his stepmother said, wanting *'wealth was striving after wind.'*

Shirin read his face. "She had no money?"

"None—" he replied, remembering she cried over the loss of her family, saying how much they loved her when she left them.

"What happened?"

"My stepfather drank." He ruined some car repair business in California. He was a broken stump, estranged from everyone. He said he didn't care about the other guy because the other guy didn't care about him. That was his truth of estrangement, a barren coyote landscape, corrupt with too many caring only about money. Such meanness made him angry; it crippled his stepmother.

"What did she look like?"

"Large, tearful eyes." They implored him not to be like other men. "She laughed in my childish ways too—" he said, reliving those earliest years. "She showed me how I should love."

"It's not good to hate; it eats you up and doesn't bring the coyotes to ground, rather, only gives them more to feed upon."

"I know."

"Did she have other children?"

"She couldn't have children, so, she was afraid of loosing me, afraid of meeting someone and my father taunted her for it." He knew her fear of loosing him was because he was all she had. Fear *some unidentified person* might actually take him from her gripped her. But, he could never identify such a person.

"*Who* was she afraid of?" Her eyes revealed special interest.

"I don't know; it was strange—" He had tried to equate her fear with something he knew, but, wasn't able to. "There's a lot that's strange. People change and nothing is like it was the day before."

"Did your father beat her?"

"When he drank."

"And you?"

"Yes," he repeated. "He wanted to sell me. He was crazy."

"Did he drink himself to death?"

"Yes."

"Why move from California?"

"Something about his business, some business. My mother never spoke of it—something bad, I don't know." Oddly his stepfather wanted to return. "He wanted to go back, and she didn't. I'm glad we stayed because I liked the woods."

"Why'd you join the Navy?"

"To find out about it out there."

"'Cause that's where *they* came from?"

"Yes. And *me.*"

"Did her fear of loosing you have to do with California?"

His stepmother became frightened when her husband mentioned California. He shrugged. "I'll never know."

"It's curious."

"I miss her. That's all I know."

"You never found any record."

"Nothing."

"Usually when people fear things, it's because they've done wrong."

"Not her."

"Not from what you say, no. What did she look like?"

"Soft, black hair, dark eyes like yours—" he said. "Medium, good looking, at least, people said that. People liked her."

She sat in the late September night with her arms around her knees. Her eyes glistened. "A sad childhood. She loved you. She was happy in you—That's all that mattered."

"She was sad, and I was helpless. That made me angry, and anger is wrong."

"It is."

"It's also wrong that I shouldn't be complete from her giving. It's wrong to want anything else. To value her memory is sufficient."

"If she knew that, she would be happy—" she said. "But, still her fear. She was hiding something."

"I told you, her husband tortured her," he repeated.

"You didn't know why."

"I told you."

"Something hidden made her unhappy."

"Something, I guess," he replied again.

"Something to do with you?" she asked.

"Me?"

"Afraid of loosing you."

"Not me—"

"No records."

"No."

"She suffered from some wrong done her."

"What?" He exhaled heavily. He had no identity other than his name, and there was no way of finding out with her gone. He was invisible, except she gave his life meaning. "If you only had one child, wouldn't that make you desperate?"

"It might."

"You had no children."

She didn't answer.

"Finding your sister's child has made you desperate, for some reason?"

She looked at him. *"E'yayo!"*

He sat speechless for a moment. "I've always wanted to fill up the emptiness with Gail—a home, family."

"It's all that matters," she said.

"So, *she* was right to have fear," he said.

"Yes, if you look at it like that."

He hit up against his present situation. What they were doing was the only thing he could get hold of. Gail gave him meaning.

"We aren't important, except *as we give,*" she said.

"Yes, I'm unimportant, alone. Why can't everyone see that?"

"It's slowly happening."

"Too slowly. I can't even keep my car in one piece, so what good is it?"

"No good in itself."

"John said you couldn't hang onto to things."

"He's right. Only giving them, gives them value."

"Does it strike you as strange that I have your car?"

"No. I'm glad you have it—" she laughed.

"For all the pain it's brought?"

"You can only have a clean heart, a full, giving heart."

"I feel stupid and powerless, like a newt crawling from one stone to the next."

"You're learning to be a *human being;* that we are brothers and sisters; what we call the Creator and the Earth Mother are to each other. You are finding who you are in the Circle of Life. That is the right way; none above or below another. And the car! *That was a ride!* You were doing something," she suddenly laughed again. She held the fish in the moonlight, and then stepped by him toward the cabin.

Inside the cabin, the trout sizzled on an open grill in the fireplace. At the table, he thought about what she said, feeling a mixture of relief and paralysis. When the fish was cooked, it steamed lightly browned on the table; the wafered meat, smooth as *Camembert,* melted on his tongue and lifted his spirits in the flickering firelight, which stole through the room like a deaf person. He wanted to be in the natural way; wanted those numbers to reveal themselves. "And how are we going to find those other numbers?" The question had stuck with him all the way up here.

She lifted her eyes and put her arms on the table. "They'll reveal themselves."

"Is that faith?"

"No. It's the way things work out."

"But, you don't know how?"

"You can't know that."

"That's when you said you know, but you don't know how things will end?"

"Yes. Tell me, they were college roommates, weren't they? They kept nothing from one another." She referred to what Candy had told him about Gail.

A sinister feeling grew in him and his chest tightened as if he breathed ammonia, the feeling pushing the search for the numbers out of his mind. The reality of her pain gripped him. "Knowing sends ripples of hate through me." How could she not *hate* searching for her nephew, not knowing if he was dead or alive, clinging to the hope that Drago knew where he was, and that he had not ruined him; living with the knowledge that that lost child she had lost and those moments—years—could never be.

The shadows in the room filled him with pity for her and for Gail because you couldn't blame a woman for trying to save a child even if it wasn't hers but her sister's, and pity for Gail for trying to keep from being raped; nor could you blame a person for resisting a mugging, or, even like John, for being poor, or blame a child, like Gail, for being molested—Trying to save her, was to save himself. "They kept nothing from each other," he answered of Gail and Candy.

She seemed to read his thoughts. "Coyote has made an orphan of my nephew, who only knew the cradle board, but briefly—But I cannot hate for it, *only grieve.*" She drifted through the small room like a bird on the currents of instinct and hope in pursuit of that child.

"How could you have *'dropped'* him like that? How did you happen to have him, anyway?" he asked, feeling the question was unintentionally cruel, but he remembered she said she had had the kid and left him with a woman.

"John was gone. My sister May was dying from the childbirth. I had taken the boy from the hospital. He was mine." Her eyes glowed intensely, as she struggled with self-doubt after all the years. "I tortured myself. But, Drago was after me and I couldn't hold on, or, run into some alley—It didn't happen that way. The woman sat in front of her house on a street without alleys. I dropped him into her arms and slipped into a passing car. It was only a moment, and I've relived it in every passing woman with an infant in her arms. When I looked back Drago was yelling at her, and I could still smell his gun smoke. When I came back they were gone. Would you rather I held on to the baby and he took a slug!"

"I'm sorry." He wanted to take his question back. "Your sister didn't make it then?"

She shook her head sadly. "No. But, I learned how to shoot after that!" she cried as though it had happened yesterday. "It took a long time before I came up here to try to find John, but now I have found him, and our nephew will be next," she declared with renewed resolve.

"Is that why he always calls me *nephew?*"

She looked quickly at him—"Yes," she paused, "that boy's the last of my family. *He must live.*"

"And his name?" Kyle asked seeing a strength in her of flowers and sand.

She looked intently over the table into his eyes. *"Soaring Eagle."*

Her gaze drew him in—"You said you would find him."

Her eyes filled with tears. "I lost him, and I *will* find him."

"Would you know his face?" he asked, touched by her sadness.

"I see him lying on the cradle board in my dreams—that little warrior lying on the cradleboard. But, faces change. Life changes the way people look. Yet, I will know him after all these years," she concluded with a far away look.

"By instinct?" He knew little of what a mother or woman would know about a baby—

"The Earth Mother will give him back to us," she only said with a close expression in her eyes. "I told you, you have a *Sioux* look." She then turned away as though annoyed with herself for saying that.

He was struck. "No, I look *Greek*—" he repeated, clinging to the memory of his stepmother. "John and Gail both say so." They compared him to the statue in her suite at the Sagamore.

"John said you look *Native,*" she corrected him. "I think you do too."

"Did he tell you that?"

"Yes."

"It's true, then—" he admitted. Why had it slipped his mind? Why hadn't he wanted to admit it?

"So, what does a Greek look like?" she asked, turning around. "A Greek nose is straight; you have a curved nose."

"Straight black hair." He tried to say.

"Long like a Sioux's," she asserted of his hair without a part. "Why do you wear it like that?"

"It feels better this way. I don't like it cut, it's like I'm bald."

"Why did she cut it? You should have a feather. You remind me of an uncle of mine. You remind me of my sister." She pulled the feather from her hair and stuck into his hair. She laughed.

He sat there with the feather in his hair, amazed. He smiled. "Thank you for that."

She was light, playful. "I rule nothing out. Now, you look like a Sioux, a human being. You don't know who you are, but now you do. *I'll adopt you."* She laughed again.

He felt wanted and agreeable. They were sharing their losses. "Good, adopt me." He held her eyes.

Her eyes did not leave his. *"I will—"*

The cabin was silent. He felt a stab of purpose, wanting to be back on the road.

He held her gaze. She knew a lot. He recalled when he first saw her at the shop that he sensed she'd been there before. He now knew the car belonged to her and John. She had also followed Drago for twenty years, or longer; had been in insurance for a long time; and she knew about Stick. He thought, briefly, if she followed Drago for those years, she likely knew about his marriage to Gail's mother, and about Gail herself. She, perhaps, even knew about him; possibly even saw Gail and him together.

"You knew Gail from the first," he said.

"The first?"

"When Drago married her mother, and she was a child."

"Yes. Drago married her mother and cashed her husband's insurance after his death in a car accident."

"You knew Gail?" he repeated.

"Lonely and frightened. Something wrong with her. Drago. What goes on behind doors? When her mother killed herself, I knew the cause. Drago moved them to the Valley, and I saw Gail go away to school after her mother's death."

"You saw us together—"

"Yes, back there and here. I followed Drago here a couple of times. But, it was a surprise you ended up with the car."

"Murphy's buying it for me."

"Surprise. But, then it fits. Drago's crimes started out here."

"You'd been to my shop."

"And knew where you lived," she affirmed.

"You never bumped into John."

"No, though I looked, even came up here, as I told you."

"Will she get over it?"

"Gail? Yes, with your help."

"Tell me about John's family."

"They live on the *Baie des Chaleurs* where we're going. I never met them. We married out west, and Drago ruined us out there."

"And you could never trace the woman? Why did he pay her off?"

"John knew about his drugs. If I surfaced, Drago had the child. He knew my sister was dead, and he failed to kill me, so he had the child. He put all three of us away. Our family." Her eyes were steady. Her face was tired.

"Can we *ground* Drago?" His heart began to race.

She didn't answer. Her eyes rested on the marriage portrait on the wall.

"How far do think John's gotten now?" he asked.

"Somewhere near. We must watch." Intuition guided her.

"Did you expect to see him again?"

She had a warm gleam in her eyes on looking away from the portrait and back at him. "Yes—The Circle turns."

This couple grew closer to him than any other people he knew. He wanted to be closer to them still.

"Met John at a *pow-wow*—!" she laughed, tears lightly filming her eyes.

He didn't know why he thought of it. "Drago said he was an *Altar Boy*. Something like *'don't mess with the Altar Boy. You'll regret messing with the Altar Boy.'* What did he mean?"

"*I have power over you.* You spoke of Mother Teresa, but there's another side to it." Her eyes expressed intense pain, the kind of pain that comes of years of suffering.

"What side?"

"*Power* and *violence* stemming from the *Politics Of Impurity*, or *the Doctrine of Original Sin*, which spawned a celibate clergy and made women property. So the *Altar Boy*, as Drago calls himself, who, like every small-time hood who thinks his girl is *his*, can molest a female child without guilt. That's the opposite of what Saint Paul said about *marriage being a covenant (co, together + ova, egg + an, man) between equals*, and *seeking the other person's advantage over your own.*" She then added with a wry laugh, "and of the clergy, *better to marry than burn-*"

Her words brought him a new understanding.

"Where did you learn this stuff?"

"Don't ask."

For the first time, he saw that the meaning of the word *Justice* referred to *Relationships,* and that in *Justice* was found the origin of *Freedom*. What he had always glimpsed as abstractions before became realities now. "And *Democracy,* based on *Equality,* which is supposed to protect the rights of all?" he questioned.

"Is thus *Female* in origin according to *Natural Law,*" she stated unequivocally, "something that wouldn't have been possible without first *separating* Church and State."

The following morning lakes Rich and Harris fell away behind them on 28N as the Cobra flew west to Route 30. Kyle's foot grew heavier on the pedal, and Shirin's unsmiling steel-hued eyes rested on the passing trees. Her look was almost feline, panther-like, as she rolled back the turquoise bracelet inadvertently revealing a ragged scar.

"How did you get that?" He held the wheel with the fingers of his left hand, despite the shoulder cast, which nearly immobilized him, and touched her arm.

"The bullet I gave my nephew up for." She pushed the band back over the scar.

Kyle took a deep breath and let up on the pedal. The car began a long climb, and Long Lake streamed away behind them. It was painful to imagine her desperation in putting that baby into a strange woman's lap like that. He switched his mind back to the present and the car, having to get back into the body and spirit of it like a horseman with a rocky road ahead of him. He felt like a warrior must feel in doing something right, because his search for Gail took on the larger dimensions of love, freedom, and democracy Shirin had spoken of.

He listened to the hiss of the super-chargers and felt the stiff resilience of the shocks and springs, the grip of the radials, trying, as he drove, to make even the car's skin his own, knowing he would need every resource in what they both, rather all three of them, were trying to do. He then resisted pressuring the pedal, feeling secure the car would respond when he needed it and pushed one of Gail's favorite pieces, Tchaikovsky's *Pathetique,* into the tape deck. The music was so quiet he could hardly hear it. It rose sad and exploratory like willows stirring before a storm. Quiet, ominous, sweet as blooming flowers—the melody of lilac, the melody of unrequited or lost love—The music reminded him of her *terra cottas,* which hid her dark secret in their expressions, which, before now, had seemed to see everything there was to see without revealing what it was they were seeing.

He looked to see the effect of the music on Shirin, almost wishing that he had slid in the flute music or some drumming which brought peace rather than the melancholy of Tchaikovsky which darkened the spirit so; but, her eyes followed the horizon where the red September dawn met the blue sky, her lips in a firm smile, her swallow-winged lashes, tapered and fluid, still expressing last night's intensity. The music didn't lighten her mood, as he looked into the rear-view and saw the Jaguar four car-lengths behind them and growing in his mirror. His hands tightened on the wheel.

"We've got company!" he said, his skin itching on the back of his neck, wondering what she would do, only to see the Ruger come out of her bag and her fit a piece of rifling to the barrel, not looking around or saying anything, seeming to know the following car without seeing it.

Shots from the Jaguar whistled by the open cockpit.

"Bring them bye and I'll close their circles." Deadly calm, she looked, unblinking, ahead.

He put the pedal to the floor and whipped the wheel, sending the Cobra around in a screech of rubber head on with the Jaguar and floored it. Bullets pierced the chrome roll bar above his head, and the Jaguar rocketed past them. He whipped the car around again. She held the Ruger, her nails gleaming against the blue barrel of the pistol.

She rolled down the window. *"Pass them!"*

He bore down on the Jaguar, and, as he whipped the Cobra past it, snapping across its tail, the Ruger popped, sending the tan car against the rear of the Cobra and into the trees behind them. When he looked back, fire and smoke billowed above the trees, and he eased back into his own lane, his face covered with sweat, his hands light on the wheel. "They nearly took us with them." He eased back against the seat, trying to visualize his fender, hoping he still had a rear bumper.

"A trade for the Mustang." She looked back at the burning wreck, growing smaller in the distance. "Take Route 3 to Potsdam," she said, as they sped up a long dogleg to Route 3 at Tupper Lake.

"How'd they find us," he asked, turning north and pushing the car again.

"Don't know." Two eggbeaters screamed down the highway toward them and flashed past. A few miles down the road she pointed to a diner in Piercefield. "Let's see if there's a TV."

They watched the police at the scene of the burning car on the television news. Two men stood near the scorched ragtop as it smoked below an embankment.

"They'll get another car," she said.

"Now what?"

She wiped her lips with a napkin. "We'll take the cut-off at 68 for Canton, 310 to Massena, detour Potsdam, and come into Trout River on 122 at Covington above Malone. From there, we'll go northeast around Montreal for Quebec City."

Kyle put $5.00 on the counter. He looked in the mirror above the cash register when she nudged his elbow and saw the grey Acura with California plates parked behind his car and two men inspecting the Cobra's back end on the passenger's side.

"Finish your coffee," she said as the men came toward the diner, and Shirin slid off her stool and left through a side door.

The two men, tall, slow moving types with graying hair and bloodhound-like faces, came into the diner and took a booth behind him. He sipped his coffee, having no idea who they were. His eyes found his car in the mirror again, and he stood up, and, without looking at the men in the booth, walked out of the diner.

The midday heat from the asphalt struck him in the face. He slid wordlessly into the driver's seat beside Shirin and twisted the key. A faint hissing came from behind his car. The men came back out of the diner after him. He popped the Cobra into gear and gained the highway. The Acura began to follow, then stopped.

"They can't roll on rims," she said smiling, pushing a hunting knife into a sheath strapped to her calf.

In twenty minutes they were on Route 56 for Potsdam, and Kyle eased back on the pedal. On 68 for Canton, the sun leaned toward mid-afternoon, producing faint shadows on the road. On 310 heading north to Madrid, Potsdam lay to the southeast. "How did John meet Drago?" He wanted to know what she knew. He thought about how their meeting had set these events in motion. It was somehow fateful how one man's meeting another could affect so many lives.

"He was a mechanic in Perce'. Drago offered him a job out west. I thought you knew." Her voice was soft and sad. True, she added nothing to what he didn't already know. "He knew nothing about him. He took a chance to travel."

That's what he wanted to know. Not how, but why he fell in with Drago. "He had a sense of adventure."

"That is why I love him. He is also good."

"Good—"

"He is my other part. And I am his."

They came back onto 56 at Raymondville to 37 around Massena. His fingers grew numb on the wheel. As the light slanted across the lid of the car, they stopped in Massena for gas. "Where *is* John from?" he asked at the side of the car, as the smell of gasoline blew across it.

"Restigouche," she answered.

A pick-up pulled in on the opposite side of the pumps. Her eyes darted past it at the road. Her voice was tight. *"Stick."*

The 959 and the square-jawed Stick with that shock of hair passed behind the pick-up on the other side of the pumps. The Turbo's tail disappeared behind a tractor-trailer coming in the opposite direction. He hung up the hose. Silent fury built in him at sight of the man. He slipped behind the wheel and flicked on the radio. The Neil Diamond song made him yearn for Gail.

Look from where we came/ We danced until dawning became a brand new day/ September Mornings always make me feel that way.

Shirin flung the door open and ducked behind the car. She came back with something in her hand. She handed him a bug. "Where'd this come from?"

"The Acura at Gail's apartment! And, they checked it out at the diner." When he saw the car from her bedroom window, it had to have been making a second pass.

"That Jag and the Acura were locked onto it!"

He hit the pedal and the radials squeaked. Two miles up on 37 signs appeared for a divided highway. It became a double lane another eleven miles farther on. He flicked on his lights. She pointed to a dirt road. "Take that right."

He geared down. The road dipped into the woods and snaked through the trees. As he drove in a circle, drawing the trees toward them on their way back out, she flung the bug into the darkness.

Route 30 opened ahead of the Cobra's lights when they reached Constable beyond Fort Covington to Trout River and the Canadian border. It was a deserted stretch of road, and motel lights blinked faintly ahead of them. As they began to pass, the 959 appeared at the far end of the drive in front of the units.

"He drove like hell!" Her Ruger gleamed in the dash lights. "He can't trail us to Perce'. He's got a lair somewhere," she said, her eyes riveted on the motel.

He stopped the car and squinted in the darkness, trying to see Stick near the car. "We played into his hands—"

"Coyote was following the others." She spoke calmly, trying to see the man.

The dim light in the phone booth silhouetted his white hair as he slouched over the phone.

"Back up, kill the lights," she said.

He backed the car up, and the tires found the shoulder firm.

She slipped her bracelet and rings off and screwed the silencer back on the Ruger, stepped out of the car and sighted the pistol over the open door, but, before she could get a shot off, Stick was off the phone, and the Turbo's headlights appeared on the road, its taillights flashing in the dark away from them.

She jumped back into the car.

A quarter mile without lights, they kept the Turbo's tail in view until it turned off a couple of miles up the road, then pulled into a narrow access. The damp woods draped them like a wet quilt. Kyle stuck a flashlight in his jeans and held the shotgun. As his eyes adjusted to the dark, she looped a pair of infrared goggles around her neck and began walking ahead of him toward a farmhouse.

"Is Gail there?" he whispered, unable to see the Turbo, but hearing the ticking of its cooling engine a few yards up the path.

"Wait behind the house," she whispered. She handed him her Ruger. "Plug him, if he comes out."

They then walked silently toward a second story porch at the back of the house. She hung noiselessly from the bottom of the porch, then, was up over the railing and at a window.

The quiet night engulfed him.

He barely breathed, listening for her footsteps in the house. Frogs croaked in the distance, and acorns fell from the oaks behind him in the dark. The Ruger was heavy in his hand. He might have been a mannequin in a gun-shop window, standing there, barely breathing, holding the two guns, one clinched in the fingers of his left hand below the cast, and the shotgun in the grip of his right hand, the safety off, feeling that his past, present, and future were in her hands. Minutes ticked by, and he mentally stood on the deck of his cruiser with the waves gently rolling the ship, as he looked far off across the moonlit sea to where the churning water met the broad sky of the Pacific. He then held a drink on shore leave, meeting Gail for the first time in that bar, the smell of her perfume blending with the smell of the sea, making him a little dizzy—

"Where is she, *nephew*?"

He jumped. "*John!*" he exclaimed in a hoarse whisper. "In the house-" He regained his breath.

"C'mon." John started toward the front of the house.

When they got to the front, glass broke behind the door. John twisted the knob. Unable to open it, he flew at the door with his feet. Inside, a body hit the floor heavily in the dark. "Flashlight, *nephew*." He snapped on his light. Shirin and John stood together. Shirin held her arm, her long hair hanging over her shoulders. Kyle's flashlight flew along the wall, and he flicked the switch at the side of the door. A ceiling light went on. Stick lay unconscious. His left leg bent under him; his Glok 10 lay near an overturned chair. Blood ran from his nose and mouth. Shirin dropped a fireplace poker and took the Ruger from him.

"Your arm—" Kyle said.

"Throw him in the back of the Dodge?" John asked his wife—

"Tie him on the Cobra!" she said in some pain.

"Where's Gail?" he asked.

Shirin shook her head—"The kerchief still says Perce'." She looked around the room. "But, she might have been here—"

They scanned the room. The farmhouse smelled of mildew like the one he had lived in. He pulled open a half-opened drawer and found Gail's 38. "She was here!"

Shirin picked up the gun—

"Yeh," John said.

Shirin nodded. "He disarmed her here—"

"They could still be here—"

"Not for the ten hours I've been watching," John said.

"He still wants the car."

"Did Stick tell him—"

"Stick saw the wreck before he passed us in Massena. Let's stay with our plan. Get the coyote on the car."

"I'd rather open his windpipe," John said, looking down at the unconscious man.

"The Acura's behind us, John."

"The same Acura as at the hotel, *nephew*?" John asked.

"Yes," he answered.

"I'll tie coyote on."

"We'll meet in Mont-Joli," Shirin said.

After midnight, on Route 30 below Trout River, Stick lay spread-eagled over the back of the car, his knees tied to the fenders, and his hands tied to the door handles. His hooded head was wedged between the seats.

Shirin half-turned. Her eyes rested on the man's hooded face. "Who hired you to kill Irma on the Digital job?"

The hood muffled the man's voice. He began to choke. "I'd have cut your throat in that New York hotel room, Sweetwillow."

"Bad luck."

Stick raised his head, his breath sounding asthmatic through the hood. The car swayed. *"I'll kill you."*

"Who hired you?" she repeated.

Stick laughed.

The sign for Trout River flashed by.

"You'll barbecue!"

Stick continued to laugh.

"Skunk!"

The steering went soft. Kyle guided the car off the road. "It's flat," he shouted, kneeling by the tire. He heaved up the trunk and jammed a tree-branch under it to hold it open.

"Son-of-a-bitch, Centradapoulis!" Stick barked, his head wedged behind the passenger's seat.

Kyle took a jack and lug wrench from the trunk, worked the lugs lose, and jacked up the back end. The lugs fell into the sand and he pulled the wheel off, lifted the spare out, and rolled the flat into the trunk. He hung the spare on the lug bolts and spun the nuts. As he let the trunk back down, a car revved down the road toward them, its lights growing fast and large. Automatic pistol fire opened up from it. He dived over the bank behind the Cobra. The car roared by them. *"The Ferrari!"* he yelled, as it did a U-Y in the near distance. Its lights blossomed again toward them.

"Shirin, the Ferrari! Don't shoot!" he shouted, as the Cobra tore onto the highway, and Shirin's Ruger spewed fire at the returning car.

"Stay down!" she yelled back, as the Ferrari tore past.

"Kyle!" Gail yelled as the Ferrari's taillights faded to a curve back up the road.

Kyle ran out onto the road. Shooting came from behind the curve. He stood helplessly in the middle of the road. The Cobra's lights flashed back around the curve toward him. It came in a roar and stopped next to him with Stick still pinned on the half-open trunk. He ran up to the car.

"She's all right—" Shirin looked back up the road behind her. *"He's running again—"*

"He wasn't up there!"

The night was suddenly quiet.

He looked at the shot out windshield, and at the lid ripped open up through the passenger's side. The fenders were riddled with bullet holes. Groaning, Stick lay like a black blot on the red trunk. Kyle leaned against the side of the car, feeling dizzy. He gazed blankly at Shirin behind the wheel when lights appeared around the curve.

"It's not them," she said, looking in the side view—

"No," he agreed.

The Dodge stopped next to them, and a van pulled in behind it. Its doors banged open and men ran up to them.

"The Ferrari went by me!" John yelled.

Shirin stood against the open door of the Cobra. "He's on his way up now—"

"Look at your car, Kyle!" John said, turning toward him. "Was she—?"

"Yes!" he exclaimed. *"Let's go, Shirin!"*

"No," she restrained him.

"Why? *They'll get away!"*

"You don't want an accident, *nephew*," John agreed with his wife.

His eyes found Stick on the trunk. "Get him off!" he said angrily.

The men from the van pulled Stick off.

Kyle kicked the still hard tires. "Nuts!"

"Put him in the van—" Shirin said to the knot of men.

The men shoved Stick into the van, and climbed in after him.

"They saw the Acura find the bug. You threw it out in the woods on their reservation." John said of the other native men. "They're coming with us."

Kyle jumped behind the wheel. Shirin got in beside him. "Okay, then," he said, and he smoked the radials on the road.

The median blinked in his lights by the ragged lid. Kyle's temples pounded. He didn't speak, only kept this foot on the floor, hardly noticing that the Dodge and the van turned after him back onto the road. When he noticed blood on her blouse, he eased off the pedal.

"Pump it, if that's what you want!" she said with the Ruger in her lap, her black hair gleaming in the moonlight.

Gail's cry burned in his chest. The cold wind whistled through the cockpit. Shirin was right, though, he had to be steady. There couldn't be an accident. It wouldn't happen that way. He drove steadily, the speed of the car pulling the road straight like a ribbon. The moonlight in the southwest touched the car's red lid. They sped toward Montreal and Route 20. Shirin closed her eyes— Gradually the sky began to lighten. He hardly noticed the fleeing hours, or, the dew blowing across the lid and shattered windshield as night and morning began indistinguishable.

They stopped for gas at Drummondsville beyond Montreal, a third of the way up to Quebec City. Kyle paid the attendant, and, while Shirin used the rest room, he again surveyed the damaged Cobra. Bullets had ripped up both sides of the car. The lid had long, ragged tears from the nose to the base of the windshield, and the windshield, itself, was shattered at the dash. His lights and instruments worked, but the car was totaled, raising a question about his even finding the numbers, if the car was destroyed. The mid-morning sun soaked into the asphalt under his shoes. The numbers, however, he realized, had to be somewhere in the car and not on any part of the body; for, Star would not have hidden them on a fender, a hood, or a bumper, but on some fixed part of the car like the transmission where they could be found. He shook his head. But the numbers aside, more importantly, were they on the right track in coming up here? They hadn't seen the Ferrari again.

The attendant, a short dark man with a mustache, came back with his change. He looked at Kyle's license plate. "You're the second car from the States this morning."

"What?" Kyle asked.

"California—"

"What kind of car?" he quickly asked.

"Kind?" The man looked at the bullet ridden Cobra.

"A red sports car?"

"*Qui,—rouge,*" the man answered, lapsing into French.

"Ferrari?"

The man nodded. "*L'auto Italienne—Vitesse!*"

"A man, a woman?" he asked breathlessly.

"*Qui—un homme, une femme—*"

"A fat man?"

"*Qui—gros—Un visage noir et terrible.*"

"A blonde woman—"

"*Qui.*"

"When?" Kyle tapped his watch.

The man inclined his head thinking of the hour. "*Neuf—*"

"Nine?"

"*Qui.*"

Shirin came out of the rest room. "They were here an hour ago," Kyle quickly told her.

"Was the car hit?" she asked the man, turning the turquoise bracelet on her wrist.

He searched for the word, looking at the Cobra. *"Hit?"*

"Damage—" Kyle repeated impatiently.

"Damage, qui," the man said, understanding. *"Mais non, l'auto ne pas de brise'—"* He spread his hands with his palms down. *"L'auto belle."*

"An Acura?" Kyle asked, his mind racing.

The man shook his head. *"Non—"*

"Merci—thank you!" Kyle got into the Cobra, his heart in his throat.

"If Drago's driving fast, the police might pick him up," Shirin said, as they gained the highway.

Kyle's foot pushed the pedal to the floor and the tires sent black smoke into the cool September air. "They're ahead of us! Yet, how could Drago have mailed her scarf from Perce', if he was down here?"

"Someone else sent it, obviously," she answered.

"Who?"

"Anyone."

"Should we call the Canadian police?"

She read his thoughts. "Maybe that detective, Wallace, in Lake George." She switched on the car radio.

Kyle first heard Roberta Flack's song in that San Diego bar where the image of Gail's face melted into his heart.

The first time ever I saw your face
I thought the sun rose in your eyes
and the moon and the stars were the kiss
you gave to the dark and the end of the skies
And the first time ever I kissed your mouth
I felt the earth move in my hand
like the trembling heart of a captive bird
that was there at my—, my love,
And the first time ever I lay with you
I felt your heart so close to mine and I knew
Our joy would fill the earth and last
'til the end of time, my love,
The first time ever I saw your face—
your face—your face—your face—

Her brown eyes were like dark ponds in the sighing night, inviting him in a solemn glance to lose himself in them. When he walked over to her, it was to reassure himself that what he saw a few feet away was still there. She didn't retreat, her eyes never ceased inviting him, never closed him out, never changed their expression, and the gentle curve of her lips never stopped welcoming him, and he soared on an eagle's wings to the edge of her presence. A face had never attracted him like that before. Was it her hidden pain that attracted him, or his own answering eyes that went beyond pain to the promise of completeness? He knew, now, that it was the promise of completeness because she carried their child, and they were to be married.

He kept his eyes on the road, the finality and absoluteness of the guitar and the heady cello swelling his throat. They had begun talking intimately without introduction. She had driven alone that rainy night into this strange town, wanting to be by the sea. When he said he was a farm kid from New York State whose parents had had a couple of cows, and that he liked to read WALDEN in the spring woods and look down at the lake through a clearing in the trees, she asked him to replay Roberta Flack's song on the juke box, saying she welcomed living in the Adirondacks—then speaking of the Hudson River School, and that she wanted to paint his face. She asked him why his hair was cut short and laughed when he said that he was in the *Navy*; and she asked if he ever read MOBY DICK. Yes, he answered, and spoke of the Greeks because his mother had an old mythology book he liked to read. Maybe, that was where she got the idea he was Greek, or looked Greek, he thought, realizing that her putting him in the Mediterranean or on Melville's *Pequot* was her fantasy and escape, his little knowing that Drago was her *Ahab* pursuing his *Wasicun* destiny. He felt as Quequeg would have felt, witnessing Ahab's madness. Her face was as open as a daisy that night, and the world opened before them. The world opened like an oyster, and he found himself in love with her—

"You've lost her, but we're on coyote's trail." Shirin caught in his silence memories the song evoked in him.

His feelings were as exposed as the yellow birches dangling in the September light. "It's a hate crime." He now could compass physical and sex violence against women and children. Before last night, he hadn't a clue as to what it meant or why it happened, except that it tore his insides and made him sick to his stomach.

"Yes, it's a hate crime." Her far-away look recalled her own misfortunes. "They have no Circle. A man and woman start a Circle. Other men and women complete it. They make a *Community*, and that makes a universe. They stand on the *earth* together. Apart, they are leaves blown in the wind."

What John said about a man with a drum made him want to be in the Circle, but he felt he was spinning out of it without her, as he sped over the flat road toward the sea.

"Coyotes are homeless," she continued with a deep look in her eyes, "unattached to the earth. And I mean something *special* when I say he will be *run to ground:* Somewhere the earth will receive his body, for ultimately the earth is forgiving; that is the nature of reality, flowers, and the Earth Mother. That she will take him shows the sick futility of his crimes. Yes, he will be received. *He'll be run to ground."*

The road carried them toward the outer fringes of the Circle. Gail's running away from Drago, that rainy night she ended up in that bar, was probably the night she told Candy about him.

"She was lucky to find you—"

"I was the lucky one." He wished he could relive that night in the bar, but, knowing it would have changed nothing between them, he accepted it. She was there to give to him, and he was there to give to her.

"Want me to drive?" she said of his tired look.

"No." His hands had been locked on the wheel all night. He felt that if he let go, he'd lose the scent. He'd stay behind the wheel, feeling neither hunger nor fatigue, drawing on an energy beyond sleep like John said, sticking to the edge of the Circle, holding on so as not to be spun out of it.

"You are about to fly. You only need *the numbers,"* she said, guessing at what he must be thinking, her eyes taking on a deep hue. "When you find them you will find your true nature," she repeated, so that he heard her.

His eyes fell from the road to the dash and the cracks in the windshield. He realized everything: his adoption, Navy, his computer knowledge, this car had conspired to some self-realization. His sight flew to the horizon beyond the torn lid of the car—

"No one owns that patent," she said clearly. Her dark eyes focused on him as though an opportunity presented itself.

"Drago filed the claim—" he pointed out.

"He's trying to get the patent like the others," she corrected him.

"Star's widow?"

"Star registered no patent for her. He gave her the money from the Europeans, as I told you."

He drew back, not knowing why he instantly felt threatened by her disclosure. "Anyone can own it?"

"Yes."

Selfishness unexpectedly grew upon him like heartburn. He grew breathless. He tried to swallow against the burning feeling inside him, but he couldn't stifle it, for, he realized, if he found the numbers, he himself could own the patent! "It's better not to find them then, better to let them die with Star. I don't want them."

"Why are you breathing hard?"

"His invention corrupts—"

"Are you like everyone else?" she probed.

"No!" he protested, trying to control his pulse, unable to keep the lie out of his voice.

She refused to accept his denial. "You think you're Greek."

He lost his sense of security, feeling the world was turning upside down. He searched desperately for an answer. "You need lucre in this world!" he defended himself, wanting those $billions, but, at the same time, not wanting them.

"E'yayo!"

"I want only Gail!" He tried to lift himself from the ground of self-loathing. Had he always been so corrupt? Had the desire for wealth stolen into him like a cancer, and he never faced it?

"You don't want money?" Her eyes were as intense as coals.

Locked in self-struggle over what he really wanted, he felt cleft by an ax. He thought of the Threatening Hill. He was there!

"You thought the loot would fall into your hands?" she asked, turning on the seat toward him and reading his self-doubt.

"I want it, but, don't want it—" Dumb doubt stuck inside him like tar.

"You would be my *son*. But, how?" She focused on his helplessness.

He didn't know which way to turn when he thought of the numbers, Gail's pregnancy, and their needing to live; yet, he wanted to be with her and John in the Circle where money didn't matter.

"Can you be a whole person, Kyle?"

"I want to be in the Circle," he said desperately.

"Not wanting *lucre*!"

His foot fell heavily on the pedal, the superchargers hissed, and the car ate up the road. "I want a house, but I don't want to be a slave—" he exclaimed, unable to free himself of the contradiction. *"How can I be free?"*

"A $billion freedom—" she chided him.

The monster grew full blown within him.

"They sold their women. How can you be a *human being?*"

Before the police took his car, he focused on how the car would get him land, a house, and a business, and he felt unclean for what he had allowed to silently grow in him without checking it. Suddenly, he was breathing poisoned air. *"I love her!"*

"Poverty has made you *Wasicun.*"

"I don't want poverty."

"Lucre makes you breathe hard."

He gasped for clean air. *"Yes!"*

She saw how white he looked. "Only those who *share* are free," she said. "We spoke of *giving* in the cabin."

His heart beat fast. He leaned back against the seat.

"Follow proper instincts—Never forget *giving.* Those small acts of love, you spoke of—were they just words?"

"No!" He gripped the wheel. The instinct to *share!* Hadn't he always been taught that? Why was he forgetting it now! Wealth was a striving after wind! Money belonged to everyone; it had no value except when shared. Community, completeness, happiness. He didn't want isolation, loneliness, violence, and misery. Mother Teresa said, *You Americans think that India is a poor country, but you are wrong, it is America that is the poor country . . . There are not great triumphs in life, only small acts of love . . . All that is not given is lost.* Those were proper instincts. Had he forgotten it? No, he hadn't, he had to be reminded. He breathed more easily. A $billion to be *shared* should he find the numbers and the equation. He felt cleaner. *"I shall find those numbers. I'll see myself in them—"*

"You are prepared?"

"Yes."

"E'yayo! Never forget it!"

"I will make a circle of those numbers," he promised, like a man given a reprieve. Out over the front of the car, the land opened before them; it helped cleanse him of his selfishness. His hands relaxed on the wheel. The tar of doubt melted within him. This car itself wasn't his; wasn't anyone's. It was not a part of him, its metal not his skin, as he had imagined in his shop. His fingers tightened on the wheel; his foot fell another micron on the pedal, raising the sound of the mag radials on the asphalt another note higher in his ears. He didn't care what happened to the car, so long as he got the numbers and got Gail back with them.

"You're not a coyote. You never were. Nor do you have a *Wasicun* desire for her. When you find her, do not hold her in your grip like a hood." Her intensity went beyond friendship. She bore down to be sure of him. "She will teach your children freedom that will change the world." She clasped his arm and riveted her eyes on him. "Watch that the worm doesn't come back. Have clear eyes and a clean heart, and you'll be *free like an eagle.*"

Her words brought him forward to the Circle. His mother's tears in the midst of her poverty, saying she was happy with him, gripped him with fresh force. He must live for others. Not just give lip service to it. If she was guilty of something in her past she never spoke of, he couldn't hold that against her. "*I know where the numbers are—*" Suddenly he saw them.

"*You are now a human being,*" she looked at the passing trees.

She soothed him like John's drumming in the hospital room. His spirit began to heal. He'd get the numbers, crunch them in the mini, and get them on paper. "Drago will sell his mother. *I'll get the numbers!*"

"John must get us the mini."

He lost his fear. He had been to the Threatening Hill. His foot fell heavier on the pedal and, if he didn't see it on the speedometer, the sound of the pistons told him he was doing 200 mph again—and then he got it.

"You know where they are, for sure?" she asked, looking over at him.

"*As certain as the sun,*" he said not taking his eyes off the road but knowing where the numbers were. He showed no excitement, but his blood was coursing madly.

"We'll wait for John in Mont-Joli."

The road undulated like prairie dunes, as he kept the pedal down, knowing it had another ten miles an hour in it. He *made* himself calm.

She turned on him with a questioning look. "If something happens to you, where are they?"

"*Nothing will happen to me. I'll hand them to you, when we get there. You brought the mini, and I'll hand you the numbers.*" He didn't question that he might be killed. He had no fear of it. He saw now what Star had done—it was genius. He was being given the numbers for Gail. He would meet that purpose, and, then, he didn't care.

"Do what you must—" she replied, glancing away, patience veiling her face after what she had endured, showing him she could endure this, too, even take satisfaction in it as his triumph. Seeing his chin tilted slightly upward, the fingers of his broken arm clutching the wheel, the rushing wind pushing back his black hair, the curve of his nose, the height of his cheek bones, the smooth cast of his skin, and the power of his arms, she saw him as a young warrior, a man on a *pony* flying over the *prairie*. If he had been—she wouldn't say the word, only have liked him like this, *like an eagle*. The stress of the pursuit and the sun beating down on her in the topless car weakened her, despite the strength her search gave her, and she wondered who he might be when she finally reached him, knowing he would not be so little and possibly not even recognizable. *"E'yayo!"* she whispered under her breath.

He looked hard ahead, knowing she accepted what he said about finding the numbers, not uncertain anymore about what he was doing or what he would do. The car would get him to Mont-Joli, take Drago, if he saw the red Ferrari. The Cobra had its belly on the ground and would take it effortlessly because the Circle was turning, irresistibly enveloping the future in its own motion like the planet itself. *The first time ever I kissed your mouth I felt the earth move in my hand! E'yayo!* he sighed.

"Put his belly on the ground, and I'll be on the prairie again!" she said.

He pressed the pedal all the way to the floor—

The Quebec heights fell away behind them in the declining afternoon sun. Along the grey St. Lawrence, the narrow river widened like the sea, and a stiff on shore breeze blew northward with them toward Mont-Joli.

Shirin, the Ruger in her lap, closed her eyes. He eased back on the pedal in the thinning northern traffic, knowing John was in the Dodge behind them and watched the mountains, like low clouds, passing slowly above the opposite shore.

The road swelled and fell under the car hypnotically. When he found and put the numbers into the mini and worked out the equation, Drago would take it, but would he give Gail up? The hair rose on the back of his neck with repressed anger. John and the van followed them—he didn't like the possibility Stick could complicate the exchange. They should have turned him over to the police. And where would they meet Drago, at that mini-mart in Perce' like John said, or in some remote spot where he had an advantage?

He saw signs for Riviere du Loup and exited from Route 20 onto a two-lane highway going north. Late afternoon, the sun was on his neck. Shirin opened her eyes.

"Where are we?" She slipped the Ruger onto the floor at her feet.

"132 toward Rimouski."

"You're making time."

"Want to drive," he asked, suddenly barely able to keep his eyes open.

"Yes," she answered.

He pulled off onto the side of the road. As the car idled, he nearly had to pry his fingers off the wheel. He got out of the car and stood next to it, stretching slowly, bending backward, his hands on his hips, feeling that he might break in half. His healing arm was numb.

Shirin came around the front of the car. "Walk up the road and I'll follow you."

He took a few steps. Cars passed. The tight coils in his legs began to unwind as he walked, and the vibrations of the road melted out of his muscles. He didn't need to look behind him for the Cobra, for it followed him like a purring tiger. He walked for several hundred yards, feeling the earth beneath his feet, wondering how he could have lost touch with the ground, thinking that everything that connected him to it, up until now, was through the car. He inhaled the cool Canadian air struck by the fertile beauty of the land, catching glimpses of the river that still followed east. It was a long awesome river flowing with the soul of a continent toward the sea, and he had the clear sensation that the river and the sea were like husband and wife, man and woman, the male river surging forward, and the sea pulling back and forth as she received him. There were no conditions to the motions, the river gave, and the sea took. Without that motion there would be nothing, no life, no creatures, no wind. *All is given.* He used to think that he thought simply, but, he realized, as he put one foot in front of the other and suppressed the urge to run, given the freedom of his walking, that he wasn't simple, that his feelings corresponded with what he saw out there; that he was a creature of what was out there; that what was out there had made him what he was, a man who had the urge to do what the river did, to flow like it to some meaningful conclusion. His gift of insight had returned to him because it came from the earth, which gave. His gift returned because he didn't covet. When you touch the earth, you live.

"Had enough walking?" Shirin asked, bringing the car up next to him. "We want to make Mont-Joli before nightfall—"

"I'd rather walk," he said, reaching for the door handle.

"Later, we'll walk on the prairie," she said matter of factly.

It felt different, being in the passenger's seat, but he didn't feel alone. She moved the car through the gears. He took pleasure in its power.

"This car is more than when we had it," she said.

"Superchargers," he said.

"Have you always been a mechanic?"

"Always liked to fix things."

"That takes patience."

"I'm not always patient."

"Not sitting in front of that screen?"

"You get used to that."

"Patience is the way of Beauty," she remarked, pressing her foot down on the pedal.

"The land teaches it."

"All things in their time."

The river was still with them. He gazed at it longingly. He wanted to sit by it and let its power be his spirit, even, if it meant being filled with the fear of it because so overwhelming. He wondered why John went west when the land and water had such pull here. Maybe, it was because the motion of the earth made men wanderers. Or was it because they had no women, or had lost them, and the earth itself pushed them out to find them? He didn't know. "Where did John get this car?" he asked.

"Plattsburgh. He was behind the wheel when we met—"

"The pow-wow," he said, remembering what she said.

"He was young, unmarried. I wouldn't have met him, if he hadn't taken that gamble with Drago." She straightened her arms and pushed back against the seat. "Drago lusted for the car even back then."

"It has brought us together—"

"E'yayo," she only said.

Yes, the car taught not to covet, or to center your life on things; possessing brought pain and death; death to the spirit brought death to the body.

Dusk crept upon the road, and the river took on a gunmetal hue. Shirin pulled on the lights and glanced in the mirror, turning it up to the sky. A chopper sounded in the distance behind them. He turned around. Red and green lights blinked high in the sky. She passed other cars. "Rimouski's less than an hour."

He didn't think about the helicopter again until ten miles down the road when it reappeared on their left out over the river. At first, it seemed to stay with them, then fly ahead, then slow down. Dusk blackened the mountains on the horizon, and the chopper disappeared against them, but its blinking lights and sound stayed with them. He didn't think anything of it, but, then, grew uneasy. "Who might it be?" he asked, observing her looking at it.

"Don't know."

"Drago's ahead—"

"Police?"

"Possibly, we didn't go through customs."

Early in the morning, he'd been in a daze and went through the lights. "It's from Montreal or Quebec."

"Over the river, too. It's getting cold."

He flicked on the heater, but he liked the cold and feeling awake. He reached behind his seat for the shotgun. His fingers touched the steel. "Rimouski's not far," he pointed at the road sign as it flashed by.

"We'll stop."

Rimouski twinkled in the distance. She dropped back into the traffic as it followed the river, and took a right up a hill. It was a clean town with colorful buildings and a church on a hill. She parked at a supermarket beside a panel truck, which hid them from the river. "Let's buy food." She pulled the key and got out of the car.

He had his sea legs, and the ground pitched under him. They walked into the supermarket's harsh fluorescent lights. "You get some bottled water." She didn't pause at the front of the store, but walked right through.

They met back at the checkout counter. She had meat and bread, pickles, and a jar of fish. Her eyes took in everyone near her in the store.

At the car, she popped the trunk and took a windbreaker from her duffel bag. He pulled on a sweater. The deli aromas from the supermarket made him hungry. He pointed at the *Homard* sign on a small fish market across the street.

"Sandwiches will have to do." She folded the meat in between slices of bread laid out on her duffel bag. She handed him a turkey sandwich. He twisted the top off one of the water bottles and gave it to her. They stood at the back of the car and ate.

He strained his ears over the sound of passing traffic. "I don't hear the chopper."

"Could be nothing," she replied, chewing slowly.

In the car he looked under the steering wheel at the dials; she slapped down the trunk and slipped the grocery bags behind the seats. "How's your arm?"

"Okay—we need gas."

"Over there," she pointed.

He drove across the street to a gas station. After filling up, he took a left up the street and they were back on 132. He felt good having eaten and with the cold air blowing over the top of the car. "Maybe twenty minutes to Mont-Joli."

"We wait for John—You have the paper?" she asked.

He felt his pocket for the numbers. "Yes."

Mont-Joli was larger than Rimouski. They stopped at a motel at the top of a long hill on the east branch of 132 which would take them into the valley to Amqui, Causapscal, and Matapedia where the road hugged the coast of Chaleurs Bay up to Richmond, Grand-Riviere, and Perce'.

"John will know we're up here." She handed him a flashlight before checking in. "Get those numbers now—" She walked through the dark to the dimly lit lobby of the motel office.

The car was parked in front of the motel, and there was just enough light to see the front of it. He began to breath hard because *this was the moment.* He moved the light over the dash and stopped at the panel. He looked up, as if someone might be watching him, but the lot was empty in the cool night, with only the twinkling stars above the low building bearing silent witness to what he might find.

He pointed the light onto the speedometer—then let it fall to the odometer, and there were the numbers: *77777.7*. Star had programmed them to click in when he went over 200 mph. He had heard the sound on I 87 for the first time. It was that odd sound he had heard coming from the dash or the front of the car—He looked at the numbers again. He didn't have to write down six sevens. How often had he thought that the odometer was broken? Shirin appeared beside the car.

"Find them?"

"Yes," he answered, pointing at the odometer and the set of sevens. "I heard it when we first went over 200 mph, and then again when we were talking about the poison in me—*that's when I saw them.*"

"Ingenious—Under your nose—" she said of Star.

He was sweating. He wiped his forehead with his good hand—

"Yes—"

She put the paper with the transmission numbers into her shirt.

"A few hours."

They took their bags out of the car and went into the motel room. "I'll stay with the car," he said, picking a folded blanket up off a chair.

She pointed to a cot in the corner of the room. "Take that, you can't sleep in the car—"

He set the cot up next to the car and spread the blanket over it. She brought him a pillow. "Sleep, John will get here early."

"I wish they'd ditched Stick." His arm began to itch under his cast.

"Don't worry." She walked back into the motel and closed the door after her.

On the cot, he sighed with relief that he'd found the numbers, but Stick made him uneasy. He shivered with the thought of his getting lose, and, then, as if in seconds, Shirin was pulling him awake. "I'll watch now," she said, her black hair shining in the faint streetlight.

"What time is it?"

"3:00 AM—you've slept five hours."

He stumbled into the shower and held his cast up above his waist, letting the hot water wash the road dirt off him. Refreshed, he dressed and went back outside—No one was around, and everything was all right with the car.

Shirin went back into the motel. He was eager to get back on the road. As he leaned against the car, thinking, the sound of a copter rotor grew on the air—it seemed over the city near the water at first, but the hill quickly carried the sound up toward him. He jumped away from the car. *"The copter!"* he shouted at the door, as the helicopter grew fast upon them, appearing right over the buildings fronting the road.

"Come on!" She pulled him away from the door and ran close to the building out of the parking lot, the copter making a pass, then, dipping, coming in again for another run, when, suddenly, it rocketed the car.

They threw themselves on the ground as the copter dipped for another pass. She held the Ruger in two hands as the copter went over them and began squeezing shots off one after the other. The copter tipped, wobbled slightly, then, smoking, struck a utility pole and exploded against the night sky. Smoke and a red hallo hung over the empty road.

She pulled him toward the road away from the motel. *"They would rather blow it than have anyone else get it!"*

They walked down the hill toward the center of town. An ambulance and two blue and white police cars screamed by them and disappeared up the road toward the burning helicopter. A mile from the wreck, the Dodge's lights appeared, bobbing up and down on the uneven road. Shirin waved.

"Quoyeh! I thought you'd be in Perce!" John shouted as they ran to the other side of the truck.

Shirin climbed in beside him. "Look ahead."

John slipped the truck into gear.

Kyle looked through the back window. "Stick still in the van?"

"Bound and gagged in the back," John answered.

"How many in the van?"

"Three."

"Give you trouble?"

"Not with a slip knot around his neck. They'll hang him from a bridge, if he gives them trouble."

The canvas-wrapped boxes were in the back of the truck. "You've got the mini," he said with relief.

"*Quoyeh, nephew!*" John exclaimed, as they approached the smoldering Cobra at the motel, the fire so intense it had blackened the building. "*A good car!*"

"He got the numbers," Shirin said of Kyle.

"Where were they?" He leaned forward over the wheel and looked at him.

"Triggered into the odometer. The car had to race to pop them up." Kyle answered.

"How'd you find them?"

"Dawned on me—I heard the sound and it dawned on me."

John laughed. "*What a car!*"

Up the road, a fire truck dowsed the burning helicopter, and the police flagged them around it. Three bodies lay on the ground. He recognized a blackened face as of one of the men at the Pierceville diner.

"Acura coyotes," Shirin said with a fatal expression.

They drove down into the gentle Matapedia valley, where evergreens gave way to hardwoods, the morning sun striking the truck's windshield. Lac Matapedia opened north of the road on their left just before they entered Amqui. It was giving and well-watered land, and he felt impatient.

"Where're we going to set up the mini, Shirin?" he suddenly asked.

She opened a tourist guide from the Mont-Joli motel. "La Normandie, Le Bonaventure Sur Mer, Le Mirage du Rocher Perce'—"

He glanced at the modern hotels in the guide. La Normandie had a lot of glass and white clapboards with red roof. "Maybe Drago will be there."

"Will he recognize the pickup?"

His face clouded. The Dodge was in the lot when Drago tried for his car. The truck was neon green. "You can't forget this green—"

"It'll blend in with the other jalopies at the wharf," John said.

"How long to Perce'?" he asked.

"Seven hours, no stops. We'll get in at dark."

"We can hide the pickup," she suggested, forming a plan.

"He might recognize it—"

They crossed the Matapedia. The road wound into the hills, and the wide shallow river reappeared. It shimmered a brownish blue in the late morning sun.

"We'll salmon fish here, eh, *nephew?*" John said of the river.

The land with its farms and its golden and red hardwoods in the fall light reminded him of the lower Adirondacks. "We'll come back."

At Matapedia the Restigouche joined the Matapedia where it flowed into the Baie des Chaleurs. John looked longingly at the houses in Restigouche, but said nothing.

"Let's overnight on Mont-Joseph."

"Carleton's not far," John said.

"Thought you wanted to get to Perce' tonight," Kyle said.

Shirin changed her mind. "3:00 AM is better."

"Why?"

"Drago will be asleep. We've got to get this truck off the road. Our chances are better at night. We'll leave it in the woods and take the van. We'll slip into Perce' early." She had already worked out a plan.

"So we camp?" John asked without enthusiasm.

"Can't check into a motel," she said, struck by his tone.

The van followed, not too close, just tailing. "I lost my shotgun in the car." If he was going to be in the van with Stick, he wanted it.

"Too bad. Nice gun."

"What about Drago?" John asked.

"We'll take him."

"The others?"

"Keep Stick quiet."

"In the woods?"

"But, he knows where Drago is."

Her eyes glazed over. "Can't take him."

"Are you sure Drago will tell you what you want to know; he'll release Gail?"

"We'll get the *widget.*"

"Where?"

"La Normandie—" She rested against the seat.

"If he's there."

"He went through Drummondsville."

"And Trout River," Kyle pointed out, not so certain he'd be up there.

"Wily coyote thought he'd pick you off like a partridge on the ground. They do that—run, come back, run again—but, if you know where they're denned, they come back. His territory is up here," John argued, "or so he thinks it's *his* territory. The Circle is turning on him."

Yes, John was right. He grew up here and Drago had interests. Drugs and the car brought him back from California. He sent the scarf from Perce'. Denned, he waited.

It was 2:30 PM. They passed Point-a-la-Croix and Point-a-la- Garde. Tomorrow morning, they'd be only an hour from Perce'. He clenched his fists.

The road rose along the coast, and they passed one hamlet after the other. The sea grew larger as the coastline of Campbelton across the Bay in New Brunswick grew more distant, until it fell away behind them. Lobster boats bobbed in the Bay, and in the northeast on the flat, white horizon the dim shapes of ocean-going freighters shimmered like mirages. Perce' was on the St. Lawrence Gulf, and beyond that Europe. When he got her—but, Shirin said not to possess her. How hard to hold her, without holding her.

She noticed his agitation. "Relax."

"Yes," he said.

"It is the way—"

"Something could happen."

"What?"

"He'll do something stupid."

"That's the way."

"She knows," John broke his silence.

The drone of the six-cylinder filled the cab. She put her hand on his arm, the scar on her wrist visible. *"Tomorrow, Perce'."*

He breathed heavily, trying to find a place to lay his doubt. "You knocked that chopper out of the sky—They're not in the picture."

She raised her eyebrows. Her eyes revealed some deep memory. "Their trails ran out. No more ragtops or flat tires."

Maybe there was a place out west big and quiet enough where you could forget. But, you couldn't roll the clock back, or make the planet turn in the opposite direction. He supposed he might have such a pre-*Wasicun* memory himself, if she had such a memory. All people were related. *There really was no such thing as race.*

John slowed the pickup. "Our turn is up here."

The van was in the side view. It grew larger until right behind them. John put on his blinker in Carleton and took a left. The road ran up the mountain through the evergreens overlooking the Baie.

"I wonder what the equation looks like." His foot touched John's drum on the floor.

"Like sweet grass," Shirin said.

"*Hey!*" John suddenly shouted, slamming on the brakes, the van nearly rear-ending them.

Shirin grasped the dash.

"No need to go up there. No need to camp. Drop Stick at Restigouche. No need to hide from the police. Change cars. Go on later tonight. *Quoyeh!*"

"Leave Stick?"

"He'll tell us where Drago is." John jumped out of the pickup and shouted at the van. *"Back to Restigouche!"*

The van spun its tires on the shoulder.

"Why?" his wife asked him—

"We're together. I can go back now."

She laughed. *"We're turning in the Circle. E'yayo!"*

John spun the truck around, grinding the gears, burning oil, and sending a plume of blue smoke up through the floorboards into the cab. "*John!*" Kyle exclaimed.

"*His* territory? *Quoyeh! Not yet!*" he shouted, spinning the wheel and dragging by the van.

"You have juice, electricity?" Kyle shouted over the roar of the engine, thinking of the mini—

"All you need, *nephew*!"

John pulled off in Restigouche at a pine-sided house among some pines. He slid off the seat and waved to the van. He went to the door.

"Did you know, Shirin?"

"He had to come home with *me.*" A woman came out of the house. She embraced John. "See what a loyal husband he is?" A crowd gathered in front of the house.

They got out of the pickup, and she spoke to the three men. She checked on Stick tied near the rear door in the van. The woman who met John smiled at her. She was a slender woman who parted her long hair on the side. She wore a deerskin dress and moccasins. "I'm Iron Clover."

Shirin smiled. "I am Shirin Sweetwillow."

"Here's the *Wasicun!*" a man said, peering into the van.

"Tied up like a rabid dog," a second man wearing braids, said.

"Killed two men and a woman for a guy in Perce'," Kyle said.

"He has Kyle's girl," John told them.

"What do you want us to do with him, John?" one of the men with the van asked.

John opened the back of the van. "Get him out."

Stick looked angrily at the people around the van. He didn't want to get out.

John pulled him by the leg. *"C'mon, coyote!"*

Stick, sullen and angry, stumbled out and stood up. He stood a head over the top of the van, his shoulders wide as a wheelbarrow.

John jerked at the knot on the gag and let it fall to the ground like it was lousy. "Light a fire, and we'll talk with him."

One of the men from the van took the rope around Stick's thick neck. He led him out behind the house where the men lit a fire. Smoke floated up into the trees. They sat Stick by the fire.

Some women in their 50s brought out a basket of sandwiches. "Hungry?"

The men carried over a table. One of the women handed Stick a sandwich. He took it with a grunt. John went over to him as he munched on the sandwich, a piece of turkey falling half out of his mouth. "Where is Drago?"

"You crazy Injun!" Stick spat out.

John reflected. The people waited. "Going to make it hard?"

Stick laughed and flung the rest of the sandwich into the fire. "You little breed runt."

John was unmoved. "We want the girl." He nodded to two men.

They pulled Stick over to the fire. Others brought branches, the thickness of a man's arm, from the woods. John tied a branch to Stick's leg. "We call this the *hot foot.*"

Stick laughed derisively. *"You prairie chicken."*

"Shoe rubber's like hot iron, you two-legged coyote."

John pegged the branches and Stick's outstretched legs to the ground. The soles of his shoes were inches from the flames. "Let's leave coyote—"

"What are you going to do with him when you go on to Perce'?" one of the men asked.

"You can have him. But, we need a car. Any jalopies around?"

"Iron Clover's jeep—" another man said, looking for her consent.

"Take it, John Eagle," she said.

He turned to the others. "We'll leave the van and the Dodge here—"

"Out back."

They parked the van and the pickup beyond the fire. The men and women sat, talked, and ate. Shirin, Kyle, and John sat together, answering their questions. Once everyone knew what was going on, one of the men asked, "Smell anything?"

The group shook their heads, as though they didn't know what he was talking about. John went to the Dodge for his drum. He drummed a long rhythmical beat. The men started singing. It grew dark under the trees though it was 4:00 PM. Kyle listened to the drum, then jumped to his feet. "Shirin, the mini!"

"*E'yaho!*"

They carried it into the kitchen. Kyle sat behind the bright screen at the kitchen table. The board on the side lit up. He punched in the first set of numbers, watched the screen roll with the repeating forms, and then punched in the set of sevens. Instantly the screen changed and an equation glowed on the screen. Shirin took it down. "That's the friction co-efficient of the silicon for the micro machine." She double-checked it, and then put two pieces of paper into her shirt pocket.

"*That's all?*"

"Just a $billion equation." A shout behind the house suddenly broke the stillness in the kitchen. "Now we get the rest—"

He pushed the SAVE button and switched off the computer.

Outside it was dark, and the acrid smell of burning rubber hung in the air. Stick's face was twisted like a pretzel with pain. Wisps of smoke issued from his shoes. *"Normandie, second floor, Room 12,"* he was gasping—

"Room 12, second floor, La Normandie?" John repeated.

"Y-e-s-s, godamn it!" Stick groaned, his face glistening in the firelight. He twisted his legs under the rope.

John stood in the circle of light. "He's been telling us that, Shirin."

"Does he have another place up there?" Shirin asked.

"No, no place, no place, just empty land, empty land!" Stick groaned again.

"There's no such thing as empty land," John corrected him.

"*Land! Land! Godamn it!*" Stick cried.

"Thinks land's empty—*Quoyeh, coyote!*" John looked around the circle of faces. They laughed.

"Think, empty land!" one man said.

The rubber began curling on Stick's shoes—

"Maybe he thinks this is Mars," another said.

"Empty land!" a third scoffed.

"Who's with him?" John asked.
"*The girl.*"
"Who sent her scarf?" Kyle asked.
"The PO in Perce'."
"Why?" Kyle continued.
"He wants the car out of the country—wanted to *knock you off!*"
"Did you run Star down?" Shirin asked him.
"*Y-e-s!*"
"Murphy?"
"*Y-e-s-s!*"
"You wire my car?"
"*Untie me, you bitch!*" Stick's eyes rolled back in his head.
"Anything else?" John asked his wife.
"Where's the boy?"
Stick's shoes smoked thickly. "*I don't know!*"
"Who was the woman he paid off?" her eyes grew intense looking for the lies.
"*Don't know—*"
"You worked for Drago," she said.
"*Yes.*"
"*Where's the boy!*" she nearly shouted, her voice sharp as glass.
"*Up there!*"
"Perce'?"
"*Drago's got him there,*" Stick said dizzily.
"You said he only had the girl."
"No, he's got him, too."
"Is it the car?"
"*No, the numbers. He'll trade the numbers.*"
"You mean he'll trade the boy—"
"*Shit! Yes!*" Stick's head flopped back and his mouth hung open.
"This fish is about fried, pull him away," John said, cutting the rope to the pegs.
Two men dragged Stick away from the fire. Stick revived, and frantically pulled at his laces—
"*Tender?*" John asked with a dry smile.
Stick fought his shoes off, and, when he got them off, his socks seemed to smoke.
John shrugged. "*Weak coyote, couldn't take any heat at all!*"

They drove all night—

They left the jeep on the road up from La Normandie. There were lights outside the building and in the lobby, but it was quiet. "Sit for awhile in some spot," Shirin advised. The three then split up.

Kyle sat near a low bush off the parking lot at the back of the building. He gazed at the red Ferrari in the shadows. The car was like a silent coffin. If he could have firebombed it, he would have. But, that would do no good. The place would crawl with people. He measured his breathing. The upper windows were black. He heard no one. He sat and the minutes, like hours, ticked by. The eastern sky began to turn gray. The sky was clear, only stars studded the vast sky like twinkling bits of gold foil. Dawn stole as silently as a cat on the horizon. The stars began to dim, until those on the horizon went out. In the distance, sea birds flew against the whitening sky. They hovered like white bees over a dark island in the distance. The sea washed against the shore below where he sat.

One window on the second floor drew his attention. A dim flickering light came through it. Then there she was, standing behind it, looking out at the coming dawn. His heart raced. A shadow appeared behind her, and she left the window.

John and Shirin came from behind him.

"Some goons are waiting near the shed," John said to him, nodding to the north of the hotel.

"I saw her. That window, there," he pointed, "the one to the right of the steps." A porch accessed the second floor.

"Cute little nest here. All three of them." A man stood behind them with an AK-47.

Seven toughs walked toward them across the lawn from the shed.

"Look at the coyotes!" John whistled.

"Do your thing," Shirin said to the man.

"We've been expecting you."

"Of course," she replied.

They walked to the stairs. Gail appeared at the dark window. His hands sweated and his legs felt like putty.

"Take 'em up. I'll take this." The man with the AK-47 snapped Shirin's handbag from her. He held her Ruger. *"No toys."*

Drago's hotel room door opened. He stood in a silk, gray bathrobe. A low fire burned behind him in the dark room. Kyle looked for Gail. Drago stepped up to them. "All three, how convenient. Thought you'd steal a march on the *Altar Boy?*" His right fist came up fast, and Kyle reeled back into the men behind him.

He gained his feet. He lunged at the man, but took another blow from behind.

"Puppy, you've had your fun!" Drago said under his breath. "I told you not to mess with the *Altar Boy!*"

"The car's gone—" Kyle choked, blood dripping down the back of his throat from his nose.

"You little river rat!" Drago hit him again.

"Get away from him!" Gail screamed, rushing to him in the hall. Her face was drawn and her hair hung unbrushed on her shoulders. She turned on Drago. *"Don't touch him again!"*

Drago approached Shirin. *"Where is it, you wily bitch?"*

"Where's what?" she asked with steel-like eyes.

"You wouldn't have let the car burn, if you didn't have it. *Game time's over.*"

"We found *nothing.*"

He pulled a letter opener from his bathrobe and held it under her chin. *"You found it."*

"Free the girl—" she said unflinchingly.

Drago pushed the point of the letter opener close to her skin. John took a half step toward him. "One more step, fish-sucker, and she's food for the *homards,*" Drago said evenly, not taking his eyes from Shirin's.

Kyle felt Gail's arm tighten on his arm as they stood there. He wiped the blood from his nose—"Are you all right?" he asked.

"Kyle—" Her eyes were red, almost fierce.

"It's all right—"

"Where's the kid?" Shirin continued to Drago, her eyes level as daggers.

"What're you talking about?" Drago dropped the letter opener into his pocket.

"You paid her. *Where is he?*"

"The equation."

"Your mutt said he'd be here." She drew the paper from her shirt pocket, quickly stepping to the fire. *"You want me to burn it."*

"Why you so keen on that kid? He a virgin birth?" he laughed. "He's outside," Drago said, moving toward her outstretched hand. He grabbed for the paper as she dropped it into the fire.

"*Coyote!*" she said with a dark smile.

"*Bitch!*" he shouted, helplessly watching the paper burn.

"The equation's in my head," she said clearly.

Drago's eyes turned blacker than ink. He sucked his jagged yellow teeth.

She pulled the other paper from her shirt. "*Where's the kid!*" she demanded, her hand again over the fire—"This is the last piece."

Drago backed up. "He's on the rock waiting for his mother. It's low tide." He flung off his bathrobe. He wore a gray pin-stripped suit under it. "*Let's go, then—*"

The rock, 90 meters high and 400 meters long, loomed like a Moby Dick, a beached humpback, several hundred yards out in the sand. Gail gripped Kyle's arm as they walked down to the shore. The cries of gulls and gannets came across the water from Bonaventure Island to the east. Halfway to the rock, shouting came from shore, and the men from Restigouche began running after them. Then a police car's flashing lights appeared behind the Dodge parked on the wharf.

They gained the top of the rock. The gray sky was turning white. The sea spread out over the edge as far as the eye could see, as if the tide, as it came in, was swallowing the rock itself.

"*Where is he?*" Shirin yelled, looking ahead up the rock, and seeing no one.

Drago pulled an automatic pistol from his coat. "*Shoot the bastards, and we'll drop them over the side for the homards!*" he yelled to his toughs.

Kyle grabbed Gail as Drago reached for her.

Drago grabbed Kyle's cast. "*Punk!*" And dragged him to the edge where they struggled.

The toughs stuck him with their guns.

"*Give me that godamn paper, bitch!*" Drago demanded, "*or this bilge-water breed goes over the side.*"

"*No!*" Gail yelled hysterically, pulling on his arm. "*You promised!*"

"*Slut!*" Drago yelled, kicking her down at the edge.

"*No!*" She covered her head with her arms.

"*That little bastard, that homard shit, means that much to you!*" he cursed hoarsely, forcing Kyle to the edge.

Shirin grabbed Gail and pulled her away from the man—"*Coyote!*" she shouted, holding the paper out to him, which fluttered in the breeze like a piece of Kleenex in her fingers. Her hair streamed from her face in the wind. He came toward it. She backed up. "*Where's the boy!*" she repeated, as if for the last time.

Kyle felt Drago's weight against him and took a kick to the knee.

"You'll never know, bitch!" Drago lunged at her. He snatched the paper from her grasp. Kyle freed himself and he and Drago rolled to the edge of the rock. Shots rang out. Bullets ricocheted off the rocks as the Restigouche men leveled a barrage at the toughs. Shirin and Gail fell to the ground. More shots came from along the rock from the Restigouche men as they ran toward them. Kyle swung hard with his right and caught Drago in the face. A pistol struck him from behind. He swung his cast and caught the man on the neck, knocking him over the edge. Another tackled him and Kyle hit the rock and rolled to the edge. Drago was on top of him, the paper in his teeth. They exchanged blows. Drago locked his hands around his cast. They punched furiously with their free fists. Drago lost his footing on the edge—he fell. John leaped to hold Kyle, but Drago pulled him over the side with him. John stood, aghast, as he watched them disappear over the side.

Shirin stood at the edge, gazing helplessly at the rising sea below. *"The boy!"* Her voice carried far out over the rock. Her tears streamed across her face in the wind. She slapped her hands on her thighs in anguish. *"The boy! Is lost forever!"* she cried again, fronting what the sea had taken from her.

John wordlessly held her in his arms at the edge of the rock.

Gail, on her knees, beat the rock with her hands. *"Kyle! Kyle!"* Her voice floated in the air and vanished.

The sun, like a half-cut peach, broke over the horizon, bathing the sea and the rock in a blood-red glow.

A hand clutched at the edge of the rock at their feet. Kyle, naked to the waist, his shirt ripped off against a tree in his fall, pulled himself toward them. His cast banged against the stone.

Gail slid toward him. *"Kyle!"* she screamed, stretching her hands out to him, as he struggled to gain the top of the rock.

Shirin and John drew them both away from the edge. Shirin gasped. *"My husband, the birthmark! E'yayo! E'yayo!"* she cried, her anguish turning to joy. *"Soaring Eagle! Soaring Eagle!"*

"Quoyeh! Quoyeh! We have our son, Shirin!" John shouted, as the men from Restigouche ran up to them.

Kyle gained his feet. He felt their arms around his naked shoulders. He pulled Gail tightly to him. The sun's natal luster grew higher on the horizon over the sea—*"E'yayo!"* he exclaimed. *"The Circle is joined! All's not lost!"*

They stood at the edge holding each other.

"It's our son, John Eagle!" Shirin was crying, her arms around Kyle's shoulders.

"What!" Kyle exclaimed, disbelieving.

"Shirin is her sister, May, Kyle—no one could know—"

Kyle looked into his mother's eyes, which reflected the rising sun behind him. It was as though in the reflection of her eyes he saw himself rising from the earth. He clasped her to him wordlessly, and then he remembered. "Drago hit a ledge below me." He turned, and they all looked. Drago was half up over the edge, his face bleeding and raw, and his teeth broken behind his grimacing mouth.

"You homard puke, I'll take you all over with me!" he shouted with a desperate lunge, hooking his arms around Kyle's legs.

As Kyle fell he cracked his cast hard against the side of the man's head. Drago's arms relaxed and he rolled over lifelessly on his side. Kyle crouched over him. *"Is he dead? Did I kill him?"* he asked, looking up at John.

John looked down at the man's neck where blood ran from his torn skin. "No, you didn't kill him. You can't kill Evil," he replied, turning away from the man.

Shirin took her husband's arm. She smiled in the morning blooming on the horizon, the sea breeze in her hair, *"You are right, my husband, you can't kill Evil, Evil kills itself."*

"And now that we have the Equation, all humanity will have the patent!" Kyle exclaimed, with Gail in his arms

"Quoyeh, son!" John agreed, and the four of them then turned and walked away with the cries of the gannets echoing overhead.

BVG